CANARY

NANCY JO CULLEN

CANARY

STORIES

A JOHN METCALF BOOK
BIBLIOASIS

FIRST EDITION

Library and Archives Canada Cataloguing in Publication

Cullen, Nancy Jo
    Canary / Nancy Jo Cullen.

Short stories.
Issued also in an electronic format.
ISBN 978-1-927428-14-6

    I. Title.

PS8555.U473C36 2013   C813'.54   C2012-907633-3

Biblioasis acknowledges the ongoing financial support of the Government of Canada through the Canada Council for the Arts, Canadian Heritage, the Canada Book Fund; and the Government of Ontario through the Ontario Arts Council.

 Canada Council Conseil des Arts
for the Arts du Canada

 Canadian Patrimoine
Heritage canadien

 ONTARIO ARTS COUNCIL
CONSEIL DES ARTS DE L'ONTARIO

Readied for the press by John Metcalf
Copy-edited by Daniel Wells
Typeset and designed by Kate Hargreaves
Author photo by Claire Cullen LeBlanc
PRINTED AND BOUND IN CANADA

MIX
Paper from
responsible sources
FSC® C107923

For John

GAS, GRASS OR ASS
NO ONE RIDES FOR FREE.

CONTENTS

Ashes   11

Bet Your Boots   27

The 14th Week in Ordinary Time   41

Regina   73

Valerie's Bush   89

Canary   97

Passenger   107

Happy Birthday   131

This Cold War   149

Eddie Truman   157

Big Fat Beautiful You   175

ASHES

IN 1976, WHEN I WAS TWELVE YEARS OLD and my father was still desperate to please my mom, we moved into a brand new house on Wasilow Road. Our part of town was called The Mission, named by Father Pandosy, an Oblate priest who established the first white settlement in the Okanagan Valley in 1859. Wasilow Road was lined with identical three-bedroom bi-level homes. Each house had a dining room, which led to an elevated sundeck that served dual purpose as a carport, under which my father parked his 1972 Chevy Nomad station wagon. Our car was beige and embarrassing.

We didn't live on the kind of street where people were fond of their neighbours and shared summer cookouts and winter hockey tournaments. For instance, we didn't talk to the German family who ate the rabbits they kept in the backyard, and we barely smiled—although we weren't openly hostile—at the RCMP constable who lived next door.

"What a racket," my mother said at breakfast shortly after we moved in. "I heard them going half the night. I'm telling you, Eddie, he hit her. More than once."

"Do you want me to go talk to him?" Dad asked.

"For God's sake, no!" My mother pressed her forehead into her fingers, "The man has a gun!"

Dad gave mom a long-suffering look, "Elaine, I don't know why you told me this story."

"Because Ed, I have a goddamn headache. And you could sleep through the second coming of Christ."

After we had been in the house for three years my older brother escaped my parent's distaste for one another by finding work on an oil rig near Slave Lake. Six months later he returned the protégé of a fanatical Pentecostal minister who had chosen a sixteen-year old bride for him. He was eighteen years old. David didn't even meet his bride until two weeks before the nuptials, to which none of us were invited. One year later, in the spring of 1980, David, and his six-months pregnant wife, Charity, moved to a Christian commune near Lumby.

"I give up on the men in this family," my mother said. She lit a smoke and poured a shot of Kaluha into her coffee. "What on earth is he thinking?"

I shrugged. My brother had never been strong on thinking. David failed grade two and shortly after our move to Wasilow Road he was tagging along with Clinton Pelletier, a deranged product of the foster care system who was a year older than David and brimming with venom.

Clint liked to grab me and stick his tongue in my mouth or push me down on to the floor and grind his crotch into mine saying "How do you like that, baby? You want some more?" David would turn into a mute idiot and just stand there watching. The guy had no will. I knew that, but my mother had her own way of seeing things.

My mother was frantically trying to come up with some alternative names for grandma, like we'd actually venture out to the sticks to see David and Charity, who wouldn't eat at the same table with us because they believed we were going to hell. "How about Ellie?" She said during the six o'clock news. We were watching the channel from Spokane, waiting to hear, along with the rest of the Pacific Northwest, what was going on with Mount St. Helen's.

"Crazy old bastard," my father said. Ever since the Governor of Washington had declared a state of emergency my dad had obsessed over the growing activity around the volcano. And he was fixated on Harry Truman, the old man who refused to leave the mountain.

"Ed! Are you even listening to me?"

"What's that?" he asked.

Mom shook her head, "I might just as well be talking to a wall."

"Make your folks a couple of bourbon and coke, would you, Jeannie?" My dad had recently purchased a twenty-sixer of bourbon in honour of old Mr. Truman, who wasn't just famous for refusing to leave the volcano, but also for his love of bourbon and cats.

"Not for me." My mother's lips were a thin line. "Lisa and I are going to ceramics." There was one neighbour we liked, a nurse named Lisa. On Monday nights she and mom went to a basement on Raymer Road and painted mother-of-pearl Madonnas and speckled frogs with open mouths to hold pot scrubbers. On Mondays, Lisa's son slept at his dad's apartment, so after their ceramics class mom and Lisa would sit in Lisa's living room smoking cigarettes and drinking five-dollar bottles of wine. On Tuesday mornings, my dad and I tiptoed around the kitchen and made our way quickly out of the house.

"Well then," my dad winked at mom, "make mine a double." He was a well-liked guy, my dad. He made a point of sounding happy, which is probably what made him a successful salesman. For the past two years he'd been selling time on the local radio station and he'd found his niche among flamboyant radio personalities with their laissez-faire approach to boozing and extramarital sex. Not that my dad was a philanderer, but it was easy enough for him to ignore the sexual revolution with all the good drinking that could be done among those fellows.

My mother snorted and left the room. Dad, who was prone on the couch, turned back toward the television. "Now that's what I call love." He raised himself up on his elbows. "He says he'd die if he weren't on that mountain. His wife is buried there. Now who wouldn't want to feel like that about someone?"

Sometimes my dad went on about the weirdest things. "Do you really want a double?" I asked.

"May as well. Your mother won't be home anyway."

When I brought him the drink, he said, "How about we go for a lesson after the news?" A few weeks earlier, on April 16—sixteen on the sixteenth!—I qualified for my learners and my dad was teaching me how to drive.

DAD RELAXED INTO THE PASSENGER SEAT and popped the cap off his beer bottle with a Bic lighter. "Do up your seat belt," he said, although he made no move to fasten his own. I drove carefully out toward the east side of town, through the winding hills populated by apple orchards and vineyards. "Atta girl." My dad had a habit of offering commentary when none was necessary.

The sun was close to setting; tall spruce trees cast long shadows across the windshield. The world was lit in a pink glow, making the trees, grass and gravel shoulders seem antique. "It wouldn't be a bad idea to turn on the headlights," he said, "just so they know you're coming, not going. I don't think your mother would appreciate a car accident on her ceramics night."

It didn't seem like a statement that required a response and I was focused on the Bronco heading toward us on the narrow road. "What d'ya say, Jean? Is ceramics class worth all the planning?"

"I don't know."

I had been to one ceramics class with my mom and Lisa, but it was embarrassing. The ladies sat around painting planters and talking about their kids, who each seemed to have a marvellous talent. Finally my mother piped up, sounding so chipper you would have thought she was doing a laundry detergent commercial. "Well I'm perfectly happy with my thoroughly average daughter. Aren't I, Jeannie?"

"I guess so," I said. My mother couldn't believe it when I said I didn't want to go back the next week.

"Your guess is as good as mine," I heard her say to my dad when she told him I wasn't going to ceramics any more.

"Well, your mother remains a mystery to me. Hang a right here." He tapped on his window. "Of course, mystery is what keeps a marriage fresh." He stifled a small burp. "Let's get in some parking practice before we lose the light."

We were on a street of front driveways that safely stored cars for the night; only one turquoise sedan remained on the road in front of a faded yellow and white ranch-style house. "Just pull up beside it and park."

When I stopped the car he took the last swig of his beer and stepped out of the car. "Hang on." He took several giant steps away from the car then set his beer bottle down on the shoulder. He placed a big rock beside the bottle then ran back to the car. For a second I saw what kind of a kid my dad had been.

When dad climbed back into the car he was old again. He grabbed another beer from under the seat and popped the cap. "Now, I'm going to get you to do like you're parallel parking, only instead of another car is a beer bottle."

"It's kind of hard to see in this light."

"Welcome to my world, sweetheart." He swallowed the beer in large gulps. "What you really want to do is to get a feel for backing into a spot. And you have to move slowly. Don't let other cars get you all excited. Parallel parking is an art. It demands assurance and attention, like most things worth doing.

"Now, when you pull up beside the car you're parking behind you want to give it a little space. If you get too close there's bound to be a collision, if you're too far away you're just going to lose the whole damn thing. You know what I mean?"

I nodded.

"So you line up your steering wheel with the car beside you—just pull up a little. And you want to be about three feet away."

I aligned the car.

"Good. Now back up. Slowly. And crank it."

I started to turn the wheel.

"But not too soon. Wait until you can see her bumper through the passenger window. And then you want to get about a forty-five degree angle to work your way in. She's all about how you approach her. Nice and easy does it."

I worked my way into the imaginary space cut off by the empty bottle of Pilsner. I straightened the wheels and backed into the curb, which was also imaginary, the properties on the east side separated from the road by gravel and shallow ditches. I heard glass crackling and stopped the car. Dad scratched his ear. "Well, that can't be good."

He stepped out to assess the damage. "Pull forward," he called. I inched the car ahead. Through the rear-view mirror I saw him bend over then stand up again and kick at the gravel sending the pieces of brown glass into the ditch. Then he turned the bottle he was drinking from upside down, letting the last few sips dribble onto the road. He dropped the empty bottle into the ditch, opened the door and slid back into his seat. "It doesn't look like there's any damage to the tire but lets get a move on, I don't suppose the folks around here are going to appreciate us littering on their turf."

I drove back down toward the centre of town while dad nursed his third beer. He didn't like to bring mixed drinks into the car; they spilled too easily. I cranked up the radio but he didn't complain. I guess he had nothing to say. The sun had set and the sky was darkening, I saw my father's face reflected in the glass, I was trying to picture him as a teenager combing Brylcreem through his hair and chasing after my mom. It was kind of creepy actually, to think of my parents as young teeny-boppers, before she was cranky and he was a salesman.

"He's got twelve cats," my dad said.

"What?"

"Old Harry Truman. He's got twelve cats. How do you get twelve cats off a mountain like that?"

"You could probably use cages."

"Well sure. But cats are funny. They don't like change."

"It's better than dying."

"No one knows for sure what's going to happen on that mountain. Harry's guess is as good as anybody's. Turn left at Lakeshore." He emptied the beer bottle and let it drop to the floor. "He's quite the guy.

"Do you remember our old cat?" he asked.

"Funny you should ask," I said.

"How so?"

"I just did a sketch of her in art class." I didn't really remember much about her, except her name and that she was black with a white belly. I drew Sugar as I imagined she'd be now, old and sleeping on the end of my bed. A cat's a nice thing to have around; they're quiet and warm and never pretend to be anything but what they are.

"Well, I'll be damned," he said.

I drove us home, past the elementary school, past the grazing cows, hung a right and pulled into the carport. The Germans' squeaky white dog threw himself against their front window, yapping away. "Somebody should put that dog out of its misery," Dad muttered as we made our way to the front door.

"I'm going to bed," I told him.

"Isn't it early?"

"I'm tired. And I have to finish reading *Macbeth* for tomorrow."

"Now Macbeth is a guy who could've learned a thing or two about loyalty." We both made our way into the kitchen, dad to make himself another bourbon and coke, me to grab a stack of crackers and a glass of milk to take to my room. "Well, I'll be on the deck," he said. I watched him walk onto the deck in his shirtsleeves with a cigarette burning in one hand and a drink in the other. He pushed a lawn chair against the outside wall of the house and sat down. He didn't turn on a light; he just sat in the dark, knocking the ice around in his glass. When I grabbed a glass of water a few hours later he was still on the deck in the dark with a drink in his hand, watching Lisa's house.

The next morning dad barely spoke a word as we made our way out of the house. I chalked it up to a hangover but in the evening he continued to be silent, he ate dinner, he watched the news for the reports about Mount St. Helens, he drank another bourbon and coke, or three, but the only time he spoke was to thank my mother for the tuna casserole. Mom, on the other hand, chatted endlessly about nothing. His silence perked her right up. At dinner she asked me about my day at school, she clucked her tongue over the news and said, "Can you imagine? An active volcano this far north?" She didn't wait for either of us to answer before she launched into a commentary about that crazy old man with a death wish and how it was going to end up costing good money to get him out, just you wait and see. Dad stood up and left the room so she suggested we go to Orchard Park Mall to get new summer clothes on the weekend.

My father stayed quiet for the rest of the week. Mom responded with uncharacteristic chattiness—like they had switched bodies in some kind of supernatural mishap. I stuck to my room, which neither of them seemed to notice. And each night, after the evening news and the reports about the mountain, dad would knock on my door with a box of beer under his arm and we would head out for a driving lesson. He would crack the first beer as we began and make his way halfway through the case before we finished, carrying on conversation like there was nothing unusual happening except the geological surprise of Mount St. Helens waking up.

When we returned home my mom would be sitting on the front steps with Lisa, smoking and laughing. My dad would snort and head right to the basement, and my mom and Lisa would be all over me, commenting so loudly that I was forced to hurry inside.

"Oooh, there's a sexy young driver!" they'd exclaim.

Or, "There's no controlling her once she's driving, Eddie!" Like he ever tried to control me. I can't even begin to guess why they thought they were funny.

On Saturday my dad and I made a long drive through the valley. Mount St. Helen's had stopped spewing steam and smoke and dad was pretty dejected about the whole thing. "Well, it's good for Harry but I was hoping for more of a show. How about we go to Vernon for lunch? I could stand a drink." He pulled a cigarette out of his pocket. "Maybe she decided to settle down."

"Who?"

"The volcano. Maybe she's calming down for the old man."

"Oh." I said. Not that he was making any sense.

"I love this time of year." He unrolled the window to release the smoke, "Before everything heats up."

"Whatever happened to Sugar?" I asked.

"Who?"

"Our cat."

"Your mother was allergic."

"She was?"

"Well, she had no time for cats. She said she had her hands full with you and your brother."

"I thought Sugar ran away. Or died."

"Probably." He took a long drag on his cigarette and then let the smoke out in a sigh. "I loved that little bugger."

"What happened to her?"

"Oh, I don't know, honey." He shifted in his seat. "Your mother took her for a drive."

"What do you mean?"

"Well, you know, desperate times call for desperate measures."

"We were desperate?"

"Your mother was."

"Jesus, dad."

"No one's happy if mommy's not happy."

"Well that explains a lot."

He looked at me, surprised I guess, and then began to sing, "I'll be with you in apple blossom time. I'll be with you to change your name to mine. One day in May I'll come to say happy surprise that the sun shines on today."

So my mom got rid of our cat. I wanted to ask how but dad was tripping out to old music and generally weirder than usual and the drive to Vernon is scary and twisty so I turned my attention to the road and left him to his song and the blooming fruit trees.

When we got home mom was gone. She'd left a package of wieners and a can of beans on the counter. "Jesus. Bloody wieners and beans?"

"It's okay," I said. "I'm going out to meet up with Tina and Shelley anyway." We had plans to drop in on a party of grade twelves that Tina's brother had told her about.

"I want you in by 11:30." He seemed mad.

"Okay."

"I'm going out for a drink."

When I left at seven, neither of my parents was home. I poured a third of my dad's bourbon and a third of his vodka into a jar, topped it off with coke and headed out to meet the girls. When I got home at 12:15 the house was still empty. Not that I cared, I was drunk enough to want to get right into bed. This gorgeous guy named Paolo had flirted with me all night. I know he wanted me because he gave me one of his Colts cigars. I'd never heard of a guy named Paolo before, he was from the west side but came with his cousin Rick who went to my school, who was nothing to shake a stick at either. Anyway, my parents didn't know I broke curfew and I fell asleep with a smile on my face.

I woke a few hours later to my mother yelling. "Don't be a fucking idiot, Ed!" I rolled onto my back and tried to see my ceiling through the dark. I could hear my dad crying.

I wished I'd gotten drunker at the party.

There was some more muffled talking and crying and then I heard my mom again. "There's nothing you can do. I love her."

"And I was happy for you," my dad's voice rose sharply, "because you finally found a friend."

It took a few minutes for that to sink in. My mom was in love with Lisa? And then my dad was crying like a baby again.

"Are you ready?" Lisa must have come in through the back.

"Go to hell!" he cried. "Both of you." Then I heard the back door close and my dad pacing the kitchen, clapping his hands, I think. I wasn't going to touch that with a ten-foot pole so I turned my face toward the wall and willed sleep to come through my dad's blubbering and the totally embarrassing idea of my mom making out with Lisa. Knowing my mom, she was going to make a spectacle of it, turn it into some kind of show for the cop and the Germans, and the next thing you know it would be all over school.

I guess I fell asleep around the time the sun was coming up because when I opened my eyes it was 12:30 in the afternoon. My dad way lying on the couch, watching the television. "Old Harry's dead," he told me.

"What?"

"The mountain blew to smithereens. There's no way he made it out. Not him, not the cats."

"Oh."

"And your mother moved out."

"I heard."

"Well I guess that saves me trying to explain it."

"I guess so."

"Not that I understand it." He squeezed his nose between his thumb and forefinger. "Not that I understand it at all."

"Can you drive me to Tina's?"

I probably should have stayed home with my dad but I felt sick to my stomach from the liquor, or the cigar, or my mom, and if I stayed in that house I think I would have screamed my head off. That night I figured it would be best if I slept at Tina's, I don't know, in case they wanted to fight it out a little more. It was too weird to sleep at our place.

Monday morning I woke to a thin dusting of ash over cars and a hazy sky. Our biology teacher Miss Franklin was breathless with excitement over the size of the blast as we mapped the progress of destruction. How everyone could see the explosion coming but how no one really guessed it would be so huge.

After school, I slowly made my way home, not sure what I'd find, but there was my dad sitting in mom's favourite chair with a grey tabby kitten in his lap. "I've named her Truman," he passed the kitten to me.

"She's cute."

"Well," he stood up, "I need a drink. There's some sweet and sour chicken balls in the oven, if you're hungry."

"Thanks." I stuck my face into the cat's baby sweetness.

"I'm sorry." He put his hand on the top of my head.

I kept my face buried in Truman's back like I didn't hear him.

"Remember to turn off the oven after you've eaten."

"I will," I said. "Don't worry."

BET YOUR BOOTS

BOYD LIKES TO MAKE HIS POINT by opening his eyes real wide and then closing them fast. And by stressing how the red-haired girl in the story is afraid of spiders because she watched a scary show on TV where a guy flushed a spider down a toilet, but it came back up, then the guy flushed the spider down the sink, but it came back up and then down the toilet again and so on until the spider came back big enough to kill the guy. Some of the little kids are actually shaking. Bethany's brother Sean whispers, "Can that happen?"

Bethany wants to push her chair back from the table and scream *idiots*! But instead she hisses in Sean's ear, "No! Uncle Boyd's just making it up." It sucks to be trapped at the kids' table with great uncle Boyd, who has the brain of a twelve-year-old.

Boyd loves the sound of his own voice more than he loves breath. He has a captive audience made up of her four cousins on her stepdad's side and her little brother. Bethany doesn't count herself among Boyd's audience despite her presence at the table. The kids are enthralled by Boyd's story that ends with spider eggs bursting out of the girl's face. And who hasn't heard that one, except the victim is supposed to be in Mexico when she gets bitten by the spider. But Boyd's saga begins with the fact that everyone is always, at any given time, no more than six feet away from a spider. Yeah right. "Even in winter?" Bethany asks.

Boyd smiles broadly, his mouth is crooked and his left eye looks weirdly off in another direction no matter where he points his face. "You bet your boots!" he shouts. The little kids all laugh.

The girl in Boyd's story is fourteen, just like Beth. But the girl has red hair like a Quinn, like Beth's step-dad Warren and her little brother, well, half-brother to be precise. The kids believe Boyd's story because he tells them the girl has red hair. They don't even know Boyd's retarded·because he's not a full-blown, he's just a little stupid, and those kids still think all adults know what they're talking about.

Boyd isn't a Quinn either. He came with Beth's Aunt Cathy and her cousin JD. Cathy, JD and Boyd come to Mother's Day At The Quinns because Bethany's grandma on her mom's side is dead and no one talks to that grandpa, not even Boyd. That grandpa, who Bethany can't remember meeting, is a mean prick. But the Quinns are nice people who are happy to take in retards and stressed-out divorcees on mother's day.

Of course JD, who just turned seventeen, gets a seat at the big table. He's wearing a Ramones T-shirt and his hair is in his eyes but everyone cuts him slack because rumour has it his dad punched him in the side of the head. Bethany glares at her mother, who doesn't even notice, she's already half-pissed from pounding back mimosas with Auntie Cathy. Last December Bethany's mom said, "You just like to be unhappy" after Bethany told her that all of these holidays, even Christmas, are just made up so people will buy stuff.

Bethany knows that Boyd is full of it but keeps her mouth shut because one, the kids are finally quiet, and two, she wants to see if her cousin Virginia—who technically is only her brother's cousin—is going to cry. Virginia cries at everything and then her mom comes running over and you think she's going to cry too because the world is such a savage place. If Bethany cared she'd be worried for Virginia, who is never going to make her way in life with a mother like that.

While JD is stuffing scrambled eggs into his mouth faster than he can chew them, Warren leans across the table and kisses Beth's mom. Cathy is laughing but she looks like a dog when people say smile and the dog looks fierce instead of sweet. No one would describe Aunt Cathy as easy-going, hence the messy divorce. But happiness abounds at the Quinn's today. Warren catches Beth watching and throws a wounded look her way. Bethany looks away from her stepfather, toward Uncle Boyd to hear more about spiders and frightened girls.

IT'S NO SURPRISE THAT JD HAS DISAPPEARED. Bethany has an armload of plates she's trucking into the kitchen. Her mom, Cathy, and Grandma Bonnie are whispering while they wash and stack. When Bethany walks in, they stop. Just like that. Cathy takes the plates from Bethany and her mom reaches out and touches her cheek like she can't stop herself. "You know we love you, baby?"

Bethany is silent.

"Don't be a jerk, Beth." Her mom kisses Bethany's cheek and drops a damp dishcloth into her hand. "And don't brush the crumbs on the floor."

"Has anyone noticed that guys don't do the dishes around here?" Bethany gripes.

"Hey, hey, hey!" It's Warren with a stack of serving dishes, "This guy is man enough for the job." Bethany scowls at him and, as she leaves the kitchen, she hears her Grandma Bonnie tell Warren to give her time, darling. Her mother, the drama queen, heaves a sigh.

From the table, where Bethany lingers, she can hear hysterics in the kitchen. Warren, who likes to think he is a comedic genius, is on fire and the ladies are killing themselves. "And then I said: Say goodbye to disco!" Warren boasts, "and I turned Tom Sawyer up full blast!" From her angle Bethany can see him strike an air-guitar chord, "The world is, the world is, love and life are deep, maybe as his skies are wide."

Cathy squeals, "It kills me when you do that! You sound just like Geddy Lee."

Warren takes a bow and Bethany's mom hops in delight, "I know. I know. It's a great party trick." She passes Cathy another mimosa. Bethany struts past her mother, tosses the cloth into the sink and marches out of the kitchen. Yes, in a huff. They'd be dead ten times over if Warren wasn't at these things to drive them home. "See what we put up with?" her mother says to Cathy as Bethany stomps out the back door.

Bethany scouts her grandparents' back acre for a good spot to chill out without being bothered by a so-called relative. Her grandparents, Warren's parents, had five kids and these parties are always crawling with people. Grandpa Jake says the more the merrier but Bethany has her doubts.

The west wall of lilac bushes look to be her best bet for privacy. The grass under Beth's feet is bright green and perfectly cut, it springs back to position after she lifts each foot. It's anybody's guess what it costs to keep a yard this size so green. The only part of the yard her grandparents haven't trimmed into submission is the overgrown hedge of lilacs, as they provide privacy from the religious nuts that live on the adjoining acreage. A branch snags her sweater and holds her there, "Jesus," Bethany mutters.

"Language."

Bethany nearly chucks her brunch. JD is on the other side of the bush sitting on the lawn smoking a cigarette, cool as a cucumber. Smoking on Quinn land is akin to grand theft auto because the Quinns are prone to cancer the way other families are prone to alcoholism. Bethany is smart enough to keep her awe to herself.

Anyway, JD's not a Quinn; he can't be fired from a family he doesn't belong to. And even though they take a strong stance against smoking the Quinns also believe in good manners and hospitality. It's like their family motto or something, although the more Bethany thinks about it the phonier she thinks the Quinns are. Like they've always been nice enough to her, but now she's got to ask herself why, and the answer is probably because everyone's sucking up to Warren, who's the oldest.

JD points the pack of smokes toward Bethany. "Want one?" She shakes her head. "Suit yourself."

Bethany hears the patio doors slide open. "Bethany!" Warren calls, "Beth?"

She slips out of her sweater and drops down on the lawn beside JD. "It's too noisy in there," she explains.

"Especially if you're hung."

"What?"

"Hung-over, Beth."

"You're hung-over?"

"Shit-mix will do that to you."

"Shit-mix?"

"A little bit of this, a little bit of that. Mom doesn't even notice if I just take a little from each bottle."

"You take it from your mom?" Beth is impressed at the daring.

"She's always got vodka, scotch and gin. Last night I threw in some peppermint schnapps."

"Disgusting."

"It tastes fine if you drink it with coke."

"So, shit-mix is a fitting name." Bethany is dubious.

"Hey, it makes walking around Scenic Acres a lot more fun."

"I guess."

"What else are we gonna do?"

"Yeah." Bethany has to agree the suburbs are pretty dull on a Friday night.

They hear laughter through the open kitchen window and then Warren yelling, "It's true, I swear! It's all true!"

"I guess your dad's forgotten about you," JD says.

"He's not my dad."

JD glances toward Bethany then back to his cigarette. "Harsh."

Bethany pulls out a blade of grass and chews on its root. She is trying to not forget what a dink JD can be, thinking even that she should maybe leave.

"Are you sure you don't want a smoke?"

"Yes."

"Yes, you're sure you want a smoke or yes, you're sure you don't want a smoke?"

"I forgot what a dink you are."

JD smokes without comment. Bethany continues to pick at the grass; she should probably apologize but doesn't want to give JD the satisfaction. Finally JD speaks, "Do you have a boyfriend?"

"Do you live in the twenty-first century?"

"What?" JD doesn't have a clue.

"You just assume I'm interested in guys?"

"You're a dyke?" he asks like you could knock him over with a feather.

"I'm just saying you shouldn't assume I'm not."

"So you're not a dyke?"

"It makes you sound like a bigot." Bethany is on a roll.

"You're fucking weird." He takes a long drag on his smoke.

"No, I don't have a boyfriend."

"Anybody ever tell you that you think too much?"

Bethany refuses to dignify his question with an answer. She plucks a rogue dandelion that has escaped grandpa Jack's obsessive attacks on the poor weed and pulls its stem into strips.

"My mom is drunk," he says.

Bethany's reply is snide. "You think?"

"Jayzus, you're cranky."

"I'm on the rag." Bethany bursts with laughter at her rashness.

"Ew." JD peeks at her from behind his bangs, "Really?"

"As if," Bethany groans. "Like I would go around announcing it." She bats the torn dandelion into the bushes. JD smashes his cigarette into the grass, pokes a hole with his finger and buries it.

"You better hope Bonnie doesn't find that," Bethany warns. "She'll call out the army and trace it back to you." JD picks up the butt and shoves it in his pocket. "Don't forget it there either," Bethany says, "Your mom will have a conniption."

"No," JD replies. "We'll just have a big heart-to-heart."

"Those ladies love their heart-to-hearts."

"What's that about?" JD laughs.

"One too many Alateen meetings is my guess," Bethany answers.

"Fucking Alateen."

"It was their home away from home." Bethany says.

"We don't know how lucky we are."

"Yeah. Your dad just punches you and my dad— my mom doesn't even have a clue who my real dad is."

"No way!"

"Way."

JD peeks at Bethany again. He shakes his hair from his eyes and looks directly at her chest. Bethany wants to fold her arms across her boobs, which are so small that if she were a movie star she'd get them fixed, but she keeps her arms straight against her sides. Then he reaches toward her and pokes his finger into the flat mole that is stuck to her shoulder like a piece of brown plasticine. Her hair blows into her mouth. She turns

35

away from the wind, and JD, and twists her hair to hang in one piece behind her neck.

"My dad didn't hit me," he tells her. She turns to face him. "He hit my mom, then I clocked him, then he left."

I mean, what do you say to that? Bethany just blinks, fiddles with the silver hoop in her ear and considers what to say. But her mind is a mad dash of confession, excitement and astonishment that JD is actually talking to her like she's human. "I don't know what to say," she says.

JD shrugs and pokes his finger into the top of her hand. "Don't tell anyone I told you," he says.

Bethany can feel her cheeks burn. How embarrassing. She pulls her arm across her chest and stretches it like she's in a yoga class, "Why would I?" JD stares at her like he's looking into her eyes for a special sign. "What?" she asks, bugging her eyes at him.

"You sure got pretty," he says. Bethany snorts with laughter. "Seriously." He leans toward her, "I can't believe you don't have a boyfriend." He straightens up, "Or whatever."

"Jesus JD. We're related, you don't have to win a popularity contest with me."

"Do you want to make out?" JD asks Bethany.

Bang. She feels like her heart is climbing out of her ears. "That's a bit creepy," she whispers.

"I'm not asking you to marry me." JD leans toward her. "I'm not a freak."

Bethany looks down at her feet, which are tucked beside her hip. "I didn't say you were."

JD traces a finger down her arm and Bethany's back springs to life. Jesus, Mary and Joseph—Bonnie's favourite swear pops into her head. She would like to know what it is like to kiss someone and JD *is* kind of hot. She would like to go back to school tomorrow, to the library and honours math with a little secret. Bethany keeps her eyes on the lawn; her mom would shit herself if she knew what was going on.

JD leans into her space, makes eye contact. "Let me kiss you," he whispers. Bethany nods. "Yes?" JD asks.

"Yes," Bethany nods.

It is kind of soft, the first contact. A little smacking sound, then JD reaches for her hair and pulls her in close. She feels his tongue touch her teeth and opens her mouth obediently. Now it's kind of wet and there's the cigarette he's just smoked, moving inside her mouth, but it's okay, stickier than she expected, but good. Bethany reaches around the back of his head like she's seen on TV and pushes back with her tongue. She feels a surge across her abdomen. Nice.

Then they are lying on the grass, hands and mouths entangled, their bodies still inches apart, the energy between them as tangible as the space between two magnetic north poles. JD carefully moves one hand across her breasts. Her stomach flips, holy God it feels just fine to be touched there. She pulls his hand down to her stomach, under her shirt; she doesn't care if JD thinks she's a slut.

They are interrupted by the sound of footsteps on the other side of the lilacs. JD rolls on top of Bethany and they both lie perfectly still, holding their breath. Bethany can feel his hard penis pushing against her thigh. Or should she say dick? What do you call a dick during sex—pecker? All the words seem embarrassing when you stop to think about it. The footsteps move across the yard.

JD shines a bright smile at her. Who knew the dude smiled? "I'd better go." He whispers and plants a quick kiss on her lips. Then he scuttles off under the lilacs, a commando in black and denim. Bethany stays on her back, throws her arm across her eyes against the brightness of the sun, and catches a whiff of the pungent juniper of her armpit. Feels the living world across her skin.

"Beth?" Warren again.

Bethany relents. "Here," she calls and pulls her shirt back down to cover her belly. Warren makes his way through the bushes toward her. She feels his shadow and moves her arm to look up at him. "Hi."

Warren crouches down beside her. "You're scaring me, Beth." She closes her eyes. "I couldn't love you more." He sounds like he is asking a question.

Bethany doesn't open her eyes, "Why did you guys make it such a big secret?"

"I don't know." He sits down beside her, "We didn't want to confuse you." He pulls at his mouth like he does when he's nervous, "You showed me your first potty the night I met you. Right then Beth, right in that instant I was smitten and I have been ever since. Biology is bullshit."

Beth, still warm from her sexual adventure cuts Warren some slack. She says, "Don't tell Ms. Fenton that."

Warren chuckles. "Your hair's a mess."

"I fell asleep." Bethany stretches, "I guess I was dreaming."

Warren takes her hand and pulls her up with him. "God almighty, you're a mess." He brushes the grass out of her hair. "You need to go to bed earlier."

"Don't start." Bethany pulls her sweater carefully from the branches and slips it over her arms.

"If you want to stay healthy, you need to sleep."

"Warren, shut up."

"Dad," he says. "And don't tell me to shut up."

EVERYONE IS PULLING ON SHOES and putting empty dishes into bags when the taxi pulls up for Boyd, Cathy and JD. Cathy is woozy and leaning into JD. She will be content until the drinks wear off and the hang-over begins some time around supper.

"You're a good boy," Cathy tells JD.

He smiles at his mother then looks over to Bethany. Her elbows tingle. "See you on Canada Day," he says.

Bethany is casual, "You bet."

"You bet your boots!" Boyd chortles and hits his air drums, "Ba-doom, ba-doom!"

Everybody smiles, but not Bethany, because

Boyd is still a pain in the ass and she's pretty sure JD is checking her out. She doesn't want to look too interested. She is going to have to find a tight red shirt for July 1. A skirt would work nicely too. But she'll need a shirt that doesn't accentuate how small her boobs are, and one that won't wrinkle easily.

It shouldn't be too hard to talk Warren into buying her a hot little top. She'll just say, "Warren—I mean Dad—shouldn't we all wear red on Canada Day?" That ought to work just fine.

THE 14TH WEEK
IN ORDINARY TIME

1

"FOR FUCK'S SAKE!" KELLY SUCKS IN HER WAIST and buttons her skirt.

"What's that, love?" George calls from the bedroom.

"I said I'm just putting the kettle on."

"That's my girl."

September is sticky this year and the heat is pressing in on the small house, nine hundred square feet distributed over one-and-a-half floors. George tugs open the bedroom window then makes his way to the kitchen to prop open the back door. It's hardly a blast of cool air that blows through, but it's fresh. Kelly switches the floor fan to high.

"I love the smell of coffee in the morning," says George like he's in *Apocalypse Now*. Kelly grins at her husband, who has done his Robert Duvall impression five mornings out of seven for just over ten years now.

George kisses her on the cheek, "You okay?" Kelly nods and George opens the fridge door and asks, "Well then, how about some cheese toast?"

GEORGE CARRIES HIS WEATHER with him and he's finished with storms. He sings during his morning ablutions while he carefully removes the whiskers from above his top lip. He shapes and trims the beard that circles his chin, giving him the look of an Amish man. Kelly isn't crazy about the beard but it puts people at ease when they meet him. George just makes 5'10" in his cowboy boots; he's soft-spoken, not afraid to show his thin upper lip. People seem to really like that. They appreciate the George who is unafraid of taking their hands and looking into their eyes during their moment of great loss or relief or whatever it is death, and sometimes marriage, has visited upon them. He would constitute a miserable fail in an office tower where savvy and cool are required, but in the flush of loss or hope George is the spoonful of sugar that makes the medicine go down.

"Darling." George carefully peels the shell from his hard-boiled egg, "After all these years together I am still unable to understand how you can eat cheese on the very morning you must perform."

Kelly flashes him a smile. "It's a mystery of faith."

"One of many, my love. Just one of many."

"Amen," she says and pops the last triangle in her

mouth. She stands up and smoothes the creases in her skirt. "I'd best go brush my teeth."

"You do that." George liberally salts the egg then clamps his teeth around its top half. Kelly lets a shiver of disgust escape and George, happy as ever, winks in reply.

He leans back in his chair to enjoy his tea while Kelly gets caught up in the bathroom mirror. She's fixated on her face lately. George has found her checking her reflection in shop windows, rear-view mirrors and even the toaster, plucking gray hairs and squinting at her eyes to see how far her crow's feet extend. She asks does she look like her mother and George says, "I think so, a little bit," but how can he tell when he never actually met the woman? Not that there's any use in crying over spilt milk. George sips his tea then adds a dollop of honey.

GEORGE DISCOVERED KELLY when she was part of a sloppy duo performing covers of easy listening pop standards. They called themselves Brandy Alexander because Alexander played the piano and Kelly, who drank brandy at that particular stage in her life, sang. That night, instead of going up to his room to watch *Touched by an Angel*, which he especially enjoyed after Valerie Bertinelli joined the cast, George walked into the Sandman Hotel lounge. With hindsight he would say he was directed by God, and when he heard Brandy Alexander's cover of "Do You Really Want To Hurt Me" he damn near fell off his chair because when

Kelly sang the words *do you really want to make me cry?* he knew he had found the woman he could spend the rest of his life with.

Kelly was hammered by the time George made his way into the lounge, but she was a practiced drunk. She spoke slowly, as though she was considering all possible words before uttering one. When she sang she swayed and barely enunciated her syllables. Later, after George began to follow her around to the second-rate lounges where Brandy Alexander was hired to entertain travelers and alcoholics, he learned this was considered the style of Brandy Alexander.

When Kelly joined George for a drink he jumped to his feet and pulled back her chair. They laughed about the bartender's shirt, grenadine spilled like blood splatter on the front of his chest making him look like a television mobster. They both agreed that Tom Cruise really outshone himself in *Jerry Maguire* and Kelly went on about how she loved Renee Zellweger in that movie.

On George's third visit to Calgary after meeting Kelly, he asked her to marry him. She emptied her glass and signaled the waiter for another pint. "Are you a fucking idiot?" She crushed her cigarette into the ashtray. George giggled.

"Jesus George. Don't screw with me."

George nodded. "I'm not."

Kelly took George in, red turtleneck, some Jesus Christ scruffy beard already peppered with grey, glass of port. "That sherry is going to your head, Papa Smurf."

Again George nodded. "You're angry."

"Don't give yourself the credit."

"Well, I'm not suggesting you're mad at me."

"No George, I'm not mad at you."

"I look at you and I see a woman floundering, at war with the world."

"You're a smug little prick." Kelly gathered her things and walked out of the bar. George rubbed the hair on his chin, doing his best to look casual. The Papa Smurf dig was plain mean, but more about Kelly than it was about him. When he returned to his hotel room, George scribbled a quick note asking Kelly to forgive his brashness. He wrote, *I am simply a man who knows what he wants and I felt there was no harm in asking. I hope you can forgive me.*

George, a seasoned sales professional, had begun with the end in mind. He had a vision of his life with Kelly. He had no intention of taking no for an answer, because, man, that girl could sing.

GEORGE SHAKES HIMSELF OUT OF HIS REVERIE and taps a pattern on the bathroom door. "Beep! Beep! Time waits for no woman."

Behind the bathroom door Kelly rolls her eyes. "Coming," she calls.

*

GEORGE MERGES RIGHT, onto the Gardiner Expressway. Today it's all the way to Oshawa and he's not keen on driving, but these days Kelly isn't up to the task. Her hand drops lightly on George's thigh; Kelly's eyes are closed. George rubs her knuckles then quickly brings his hand back to the steering wheel; he has come to accept his own careful nature.

Still, sometimes, in the middle of the night, it's the subject of his own mortality that frightens him. Sure, he knows that God is a forgiving Father, but it comes up. Usually after one of those afternoons that he drinks a café latte, which he should never do because coffee messes with his plumbing, but, every now and then, George can't resist. Maybe he's passing by a new Starbucks, or he has a meeting and he just decides, there's no harm in a little pleasure.

Kelly is breathing through her mouth, a small ticking sound moving through her teeth. It's good to see her relax; she's mean as a bear when she doesn't get her sleep. George lets go an anxious sigh, the prospect of becoming a father at fifty is enough to make a fellow blush, although he supposes he should have thought of that in July. What's done is done. He'll manage. He always has. George knows he is a lucky guy. He has no regrets, at least none worth mentioning.

WHEN GEORGE WAS A YOUNG MAN, before facial hair, he was beautiful. Thick-lashed brown eyes, Cosmo girl lips and carefully permed hair, feathered in the style of John Schneider. When people exclaim over a photo of the young George, he answers that he was a silly, vain boy who squandered his money on Seafarer jeans and nearly broke his mother's heart with all his disco dancing. George kept only one photo from his youth. He and his mother were all smiles in front of the curved brick wall of Immaculate Conception Church. She wore a sprig of lilacs pinned to her dress. It was Pentecost Sunday, George held a guitar case in his right hand, and with his left he flashed the peace sign. That morning George had accompanied his mother, a choir soloist, on guitar and they brought down the house with Ave Maria. It had been a real triumph.

The very same evening his mother pressed her lips together as George closed the door behind him. He was wearing a floral print shirt and high-rise jeans and he felt pretty as a girl. He caught her watching from the window while he skipped to his car, tucked himself into the front seat and checked his hair in the rear-view mirror.

George was on his way to a small gathering of men who met in an apartment north of Bloor at Pacific. The group was discreet and prone to talking about Texas Hold'em in the long elevator up. If it were a two-table night more than a dozen men would be showing up. George was a popular invitee and not only because of the charms of his youth; his discretion was exemplary unlike so many of his young peers.

There were drinks and gossip and dimly lit rooms. George had a special friend he met on Sunday nights, a man named Brian who had a small accounting practice, four children and a Lutheran wife. They shared a mutual lack of expectation and a desire for secrecy. For all of his time spent dancing in bars George only saw action on Sunday nights, usually in the curtained-off bathtub of an apartment crowded with groaning and pounding men.

His own carnal nature was a worry to George. He was willful and he knew it was wrong, but oh, the smell and the sounds of Sunday night stuck with him all week. He lit candles, he prayed to be released from his lustful obsession, but by 3PM Sunday he was trying on outfits.

His mother stood in the door to his room. "What kind of man wears a flowered shirt to play poker?" she asked.

"You'd be surprised," George quipped.

She clicked her tongue and left his room.

George closed the door behind her then sat on his narrow bed. His hands shook. He folded them under his armpits and hugged himself. At 7PM sharp he left the house while his mother seethed.

George knew his mother prayed for him. She'd taken to wearing a Saint Jude chain. It fell onto her heavy chest and she tugged at it nervously on Sunday evenings when he left the house. "I don't know what to think of you," she said.

"What do you mean?" George asked.

48

"How can you play music like an angel in the morning," she pulled the medallion, "and then go out to God knows where in the night!"

George pulled her into his arms, "Mommy, I'm a good boy." He kissed her cheek. "I promise you. You don't have to worry."

His mother pulled away, "I want to believe you George, but you're not giving me much help."

That night, George came home at one AM, stinking of cigarettes and gin martinis, to find his mother slumped in her chair. There was a string of saliva hanging from the corner of her mouth. It was uncharacteristic of his mother to sleep in her chair and George shook her gently to wake her. She opened her eyes and George told her she'd fallen asleep. His mother blinked at him, unmoving. He asked her if she'd like help. She opened her mouth, she flapped her lips, but no sound was released. George ran into the kitchen and called emergency.

George's mother had suffered a massive stroke. Over the course of the next year she gained back the use of her hands and language that sounded slightly drunk. George adapted the front entry of their house to accommodate a wheelchair, turned their dining room into a bedroom for his mother, dropped out of school and learned to cook. Twice weekly a nurse came by to bathe his mother. His mother did not sing again.

George lay awake at night listening for her, for the ticking sound of his mother's breath in sleep. He would creep into the front room and stand over her, blinking back regret. His mother had been plump certainly; she loved her salt and enjoyed ten cigarettes a day (no more, no less), but the stress he had created for her with his lascivious behavior! George didn't kid himself, he knew his actions nearly killed his mother and he felt lucky that he had been provided with a second chance to prove himself to her and to his Father in Heaven. He folded up his flowered shirts and Seafarers and donated them to Goodwill.

GEORGE HAS NEVER CONFESSED his sordid past to anyone, not even his priest. He cared for his mother for another sixteen years, the remainder of her life. He supplemented her pension by teaching music and quite by accident fell into marketing church supplies and materials to Catholic bookstores across the country. Father Pat had a parishioner, Dave, a reformed junkie with a silver front tooth who made olive wood and bead rosaries. Dave's nerves were shot, so he was unable to manage delivery of his handiwork.

"Just look at this." Dave held his trembling hands up for George to see. "I'm good for nothing except when I'm in service of my Higher Power building a rosary. Father Pat, he takes orders for me, but like I said, I'm good for nothing. I've been to hell, George, and I ain't going back. I can't say it's going to amount to much but I'll give you twenty percent of everything I sell."

By the time George met Kelly, shortly after his mother died, he was managing the North American distribution of Catholic medallions and devotional scapulars assembled in Poland, he was the sole distributor of Dave's highly prized rosaries, and he made a decent part-time living providing musical services for Catholic funerals and weddings.

2

KELLY KEEPS HER EYES CLOSED trying not to be annoyed by George's incessant whistling. She knows he hates driving and if she didn't feel so goddamn tired she'd happily take over, just to stop his fucking whistling. She needs to go to her happy place, but today her happy place is nowhere to be found.

KELLY THOUGHT OF HER CHILDHOOD as little as possible, but if she had to describe it she'd be the first to admit it could have been worse. There was always bread and peanut butter (and celery and carrots for her mother Shirley, who liked to diet). Kelly went to school every day, although she attended eight schools across southern Alberta. They lived in a constant state of aftershock, in the wake of another of her mother's ill-considered ideas and rash decisions. It seemed to Kelly that a smarter person would have learned to see it coming, although, eventually, she managed to hide her surprise.

Two days before the last move Kelly made with her mother, she heard Mrs. Ledbeck call Shirley a piece of work. Kelly was surprised that her mother took it so well. Later, when they heard the clicking of heels across the floor above their heads, her brother, Shane, said, "There's Mrs. Lead Beak."

Shirley laughed uproariously. "Pipe down," she said loudly, "because the landlady is upstairs listening, aren't you Mrs. Lead Beak?" Then she slapped her hands over her mouth and bugged her eyes. "Start me a cigarette would you?" she asked Shane.

Kelly sucked on a piece of her hair.

"If you start puking up goddamn hairballs you'll be cleaning it up yourself." Shirley leaned across the table and plucked the cigarette from Shane's mouth.

Kelly rolled her hair between her teeth. "Stop acting like a retard and get that fucking hair out of your mouth," Shirley hissed.

Kelly spat her hair out from between her teeth then brushed the sticky mess back toward her shoulder.

She was reading her lines. The ninth grade drama class was performing excerpts from *Grease* and Kelly was cast to sing "Hopelessly Devoted to You". Kelly didn't even know she could sing until Mr. Lefebvre gave her the part. After that she lay awake thinking about the poodle skirt he promised she could wear. Her tongue moved over teeth, a tic to substitute for the hair. Maybe Shane would let her practice in his room. Shane had the bedroom;

Kelly and her mom slept on the pull-out, when her mom came home to sleep.

"By the way," Shirley blew a thin stream of smoke from her mouth, "we're moving on Friday." Shane clapped his hands together and hooted.

"Where to?" Kelly asked.

"I'm thinking Pincher Creek." Shirley cocked her head, "Or Medicine Hat."

"Those are whole other towns." Tears rose in Kelly's voice.

"I quit school," Shane added.

"Over my dead body." Shirley was firm.

"I got a job in Fort Nelson." Shane pulled a cigarette from his mom's pack, "I was just going to leave you a note but since you're moving anyway."

"I thought you wanted to be a doctor." Already Shirley was losing steam.

Shane laughed again. "When I was four maybe." Shirley joined him in the joke, the two of them laughing so hard they had to wipe tears from their eyes.

"But I've got a part. I've got a song," Kelly begged.

"Can't you wait a few weeks?" Shane asked their mother.

"I'm not going to give that miserable bitch another penny. Friday is Lead Beak's Meals on Wheels day. She won't know we're gone until she gets home."

"But you paid her already." Kelly was crying now.

"There's no way that cheque's clearing my account."

"Give it up, Kell." Shane spoke softly.

Kelly stood up, her chest pounding with despair. "I'm not going."

"Then you come up with the rent." Shirley stubbed out her cigarette. "But I'll tell you what," she offered, "you can decide whether it's the Creek or the Hat."

"You're the only miserable bitch around here."

Shirley stood up and moved slowly toward Kelly. "Don't you forget I can still wipe the floor with your ass." She paused for effect. "You're lucky I'm in a good mood."

They ended up in Pincher Creek. Shirley had fallen for a ranch hand named Vernon, who everybody called Toothbrush because he was obsessive about cleaning his mouth.

"You'll love it honey," she said to Kelly. "You'll never see a prettier place."

As though Kelly gave a rat's ass about mountains, and ranchland, and cattle.

SHIRLEY WOULD PICK UP AND FOLLOW Toothbrush whenever he travelled for work, disappearing for days on end. She would leave twenty bucks on the fridge door and a note—*see you soon!*—as though twenty bucks would take care of everything.

Kelly found a job running drugs for a dealer named Pooh Bear, who she met when Shirley and Toothbrush brought her along to his Grey Cup party. Pooh took one look at Kelly decked out in black tights, black tank top, a studded neck collar and jean jacket and said to Shirley, "I see you brought Madonna along."

Kelly sneered at Pooh Bear, to which he replied, "Ooops, I mean Billy Idol."

Shirley laughed hysterically; she hadn't slept more than two hours a night in the last several days. Kelly heard her mother and Toothbrush going at it all through the night—when Shirley was on a bender she'd screw anybody that moved so it was a relief to Kelly to know the guy her mother was banging.

Later in the afternoon, Pooh Bear (he was fat and yellow) found Kelly sitting alone at the kitchen table. "Hey Billy, you feeling lonely?"

"The name's Kelly."

"Kelly it is." He rubbed his hands together, "Would you like a drink? A toke?"

"Is my mom still here?"

"She's watching the game."

"Sure. I'll have a toke."

Pooh Bear laughed and pulled out a joint. "You go to school?"

"Grade ten."

"I would have put you at grade twelve, at least." He passed her the joint.

"Old ahead of my time." She took a long draw on the spliff. A seed popped and landed on her shirt. "Fuck!" She quickly brushed it off.

"I could use a girl like you."

Kelly looked him over, "Sounds creepy."

"No, no!" He laughed again. "I need someone to run errands for me at the school. And other places."

"Errands?"

"A delivery girl."

"A delivery girl? For what?" Kelly asked.

"For weed." Pooh Bear said it like she was stupid not to know. "I'll give you fifty bucks a week."

Kelly shrugged. "Sure."

It was a good arrangement. Kelly had cash for the times Shirley disappeared. She didn't much like pot. It never failed that when she smoked, panic crept into her brain, so she didn't smoke away Pooh Bear's profits. Shirley, oblivious to anyone outside her manic bubble, didn't have a clue.

When Kelly was nearing the end of grade eleven Shirley went off the deep end. After four days of no sleep and no sex—Toothbrush had recently split to Oregon, instructing Shirley not to follow—a rancher found Shirley sleeping amongst his cattle, her bare feet caked in mud. She was incoherent and damn lucky not to have had her head crushed by a hoof. They sent her packing to the Foothills Hospital psych ward in Calgary.

The cops asked Kelly if she'd be okay and she said why not? Did she want to see a social worker, they asked, and she said why? When they left, Kelly packed her stuff, leaving all of Shirley's shit as it was, in disarray. She knocked on Pooh Bear's door and asked if she could stay until she finished school.

"Til the end of the month?" Pooh Bear asked.

"Til the end of grade twelve," Kelly said.

Pooh Bear looked her over, "What do I get out of it?"

Kelly was disappointed but not surprised. "Sex, I guess. But I want to keep my delivery job separate."

"What about food?" Pooh Bear had the decency to look embarrassed.

Kelly shrugged, "You buy it. I'll cook it."

"And clean the kitchen." Then he added, "And clean up after yourself. I've seen your mom's place."

"Obviously you never saw my room. That was her mess, not mine."

Pooh Bear gave Kelly twenty minutes to get her belongings unpacked then he walked into the room and pushed her onto the bed. "Let's give this baby a test drive," he said.

Pooh Bear didn't store his earnings between the mattresses, he stored his cash by the furnace in an empty can of paint—who steals pink paint he asked Kelly. A year later Kelly did, although she considered it more like taking what was rightfully hers. If there was one thing Kelly picked up from Shirley it was how to make an exit.

KELLY MARRIED GEORGE IN THE RECTORY, witnessed by the priest's cook, a dour English woman named Elizabeth, and a nun named Sister Michael who was in the office working on an adult catechism program. Two hours later they were on a flight to Toronto, anything Kelly found worth keeping packed into a single suitcase. Kelly mailed a postcard from the Calgary airport letting her mother know she was married and on her way to Toronto.

It's not that she hated Shirley but her mother was what people nowadays call toxic. Shirley would have shit herself had she ever met George. George was not the kind of male Shirley identified as man. No, Kelly didn't hate her mother, she just accepted that her mother was an asshole and Kelly couldn't be bothered with assholes.

THE LAST TIME KELLY SPOKE TO SHIRLEY was when her mother called to inform Kelly of her diagnosis of extensive stage small-cell lung cancer, which was to say, in Shirley's words, she was screwed.

"I'm sorry." Kelly wanted to be polite.

"Well darling, we're all terminal, aren't we?"

"I suppose we are." What was she supposed to say? Was she expected to cry? Gnash her teeth?

"Well, I just thought you'd want to know."

"Yes, of course." Kelly never could understand what Shirley wanted from her. "Thank you," she added as an afterthought.

"Well, you're very welcome, now, aren't you?" Shirley sounded positively chipper. Kelly heard her inhale deeply on a cigarette. "How about a visit out to see your mom?"

Kelly leaned into the counter. "We're into our busy season now. Some weddings are booked two years ahead. I have to be here. But maybe after Labour Day."

"I'll pencil you in," Shirley said.

"I'll plan for mid-September."

"You take care now."

"Thanks for keeping me in the loop." Kelly came off sounding much more casual than she intended.

"Any time."

After Kelly hung up the phone she remained propped against the counter, letting the news fall into her shoulders and down her back. "Jesus Christ." Kelly brought her thumb and middle finger to her forehead and squeezed. In the living room, George was watching *Dancing With The Stars*. She could hear the English judge going on excitedly.

"Donny and Kym are coming up!" George called.

Kelly nodded and straightened her back. "Did I miss the Osborne girl?" She stood in the doorway and smiled at George, who sat on the couch with his feet tucked neatly up beside him.

George shifted his legs and made a place for Kelly on the couch as she moved in beside him.

"Are you all right?" he asked.

Kelly nodded, but despite herself her eyes had sprung a leak. When George noticed he said, "Sweetheart," and reached for the box of tissues. "What happened?"

"Shirley's dying." She brushed tears from her cheek. "I can't believe I'm crying."

"Most people would call that a normal reaction."

"But I don't care. I don't care what happens to Shirley."

"Are you sure about that?"

"Jesus Christ, George!" Kelly snapped. "Of course I'm sure!"

"Okay. Okay."

"Pardon my language." Kelly apologized for her outburst. "She wants me to go see her."

"Would you like me to go with you?" George asked.

"I'm not going, George." Kelly shook with embarrassment over her unstoppable tears, "I'm not going to start acting like things are different." She gulped air, "Nothing has changed. Nothing has changed."

"Okay," George stroked her hair. "I'm with you. One hundred percent."

"You missed Donny and Kym's dance," she blubbered.

"Don't give it another thought." George laced his fingers through Kelly's and turned back to the TV.

3

GEORGE IS WORRIED ABOUT KELLY. She comes across as a tough cookie but he knows better. She's a principled woman. Some people call that hard, but only because principles have gone so out of fashion. He starts to whistle that old Culture Club tune she was singing on the night they met. George would do anything to make Kelly happy.

ON GEORGE'S FOURTH VISIT TO CALGARY he took Kelly to The Keg. Before they ordered salad bar, steak and chocolate mud pie George asked "What do you prefer, Brandy, red or white?"

"Kelly," she said.

"I beg your pardon?"

"My name's not Brandy. It's Kelly."

"Everybody calls you Brandy." George couldn't help but feel he was the butt of some joke.

"It's a nickname. I used a nickname." George nodded and Kelly thought, light's on but nobody's home.

"But you'd like me to call you Kelly?"

"Yes. I would."

"Well then, Kelly, would you prefer white or red wine?"

On his fifth visit George gave Kelly a pair of pearl stud earrings. They sat on a small square of cotton batting inside a blue Birk's box.

"They're too much," Kelly said and pushed the box back across the table.

"They cost a hundred bucks." George pushed the box back toward her, "And I want you to have them."

"These aren't going to get you laid," she pulled the box closer.

"Okey dokey," George said.

Kelly laughed, "Okey dokey, George?"

On his sixth visit Kelly warned George that she hadn't really lived in any one place for a long time but was the offer of marriage still on the table; she'd like to take him up on it.

George took her hand, "I can't think of anything I'd like more."

Their life wasn't going to be made into a movie starring Tom Cruise and a lovely ingénue, but George seemed to have plenty of nothing crazy going on and Kelly was ready for a little of that. "In that case," Kelly smiled at George, "I'd say we have a deal." They sealed the contract with a chaste kiss.

They spent their honeymoon, two nights for the price of one—it was after all November—at the Banff Springs Hotel. The trip involved two acts of perfunctory sex performed dutifully at bedtime and a great deal of surprisingly pleasant conversation. While George failed to knock Kelly's socks off in bed, he did manage to delight her with conversation and corny jokes. It was good and it was easy. And much to her surprise she didn't mind the business-like sex.

When they returned home it turned out George was a bit of an early bird and Kelly was a bit of a night owl. George was usually asleep by the time Kelly made it to bed around midnight. When Kelly converted to Catholicism eighteen months after they married she felt it was time to talk to George about the sex they were never having.

"You know I love you," she told him.

"And I you."

"I just don't want you to think I don't."

"Don't what?" George wasn't sure what she was getting at.

"Well, I'm focused on my spiritual practice right now." This wasn't exactly true but it seemed the easiest way to present her lack of interest in fucking George.

"Lovely!"

Kelly put up her hand. "Just wait. Just wait til I'm finished."

George sat on his hands. "I'm waiting."

"I would like to practice abstinence." And that much was true. Kelly felt done, bored and tired of the whole mess of sex.

George cocked his head. "Abstinence?"

"Yes." She didn't want anyone to touch her boobs, or worse her snatch, and she didn't want to use the word snatch in front of George. She just wanted to be left to go about her business. "I think celibacy will enhance my spiritual practice."

"Of course it will." George tried not to sound too willing.

"You're sure you don't mind?" If the truth were fully told Kelly would have confessed to the little bullet vibrator she got down with two or three times a week when George was out on sales calls.

"I just want to support you any way I can."

Kelly took George's hand and held it to her cheek, then kissed his palm. "I'm so happy I found you."

"I found you." George pulled Kelly onto his lap.

"I guess you did." Kelly leaned her forehead against his. "I really like it here, George. With you."

4

THE 14ᵀᴴ WEEK IN ORDINARY TIME is a quiet period on the liturgical calendar; summer vacations have begun, parishioners are distracted by travel plans or excited children and Sunday mass is abbreviated. But it is George's favourite week of the year. July 6, the feast of the little virgin martyr, Maria Goretti, and the day that George brought his stupefied but recovering mother home from the hospital. It marks the beginning of George's new year. It is the day George made the commitment to avoid evil and follow the right path like all little children, like Maria, who not yet twelve years old, was willing to sacrifice her life to defend her virginal purity. Little Maria Goretti who George called and still calls upon for victory in temptation, that he may never be the occasion of dragging others into hell.

THIS YEAR, AS USUAL ON JULY 6, George pulled out all the stops. And, as usual, he took the day off work and cooked up a feast of barbeque wild salmon with wild rice and arugula. Keeping with the theme of wild, George produced a chilled bottle of Moët Chandon pink champagne and flambé bananas served over French vanilla ice cream. He was at the top of his game, and Kelly, who had been vague and preoccupied since her mother's call, ate and drank with vigour.

"Lord Almighty," she said when she took her first bite of the banana dessert, "I feel like I've died and gone to heaven."

George watched Kelly polish off her dessert in rapid gulps, like a dog at her bowl. She leaned back in her chair and stared vacantly into the distance. The early evening breeze blew her hair into her face. Eventually Kelly tucked her hair behind her ear and looked at George. "You loved your mother." It was a statement.

"That's a fact."

"This annual celebration you have for her, it's so—" Kelly searched for the word. She didn't want to say weird. "Devoted. I suppose you miss her?"

"Not any more." George took her hand. "Not since you."

"I want to have a baby."

"Excuse me?" George was certain he hadn't heard her correctly.

"I want us to have a child."

George pulled at his beard. "You're forty-one."

"So it's now or never."

"Well, I guess we can talk about it." George didn't sound convinced.

"I'm ovulating. Right now."

"You're what?" Kelly was giving George the creeps, "How do you know?"

"Well, my mucus has changed."

George jumped up. "Okay! Okay." He scurried to the sliding doors. "Would you like a scotch?"

"Sure."

George knocked around the cupboards, pulling down tumblers and the bottle of Glenfiddich. A baby! Where on God's green earth had that idea come from? Kids were fine by George, but this was out of the blue. Maybe they could adopt. Ovulating? Who even knew that kind of stuff?

"I've freaked you out." George felt Kelly's hand in the small of his back.

"A little."

Kelly turned George around to face her. "We could have a nice little family." She took his bottom lip between her teeth and tugged gently.

He pulled away. "Here's your scotch." He pressed the tumbler into her hand.

With her other hand Kelly caught the belt loop on his chinos and pulled him toward their bedroom. George grabbed the bottle of scotch and let himself be led down the hall. The look she was giving him! For heaven's sake, he felt like Little Red Riding Hood meeting up with the wolf.

"This is a side of you I haven't seen," he croaked.

She laughed, sounding husky, like someone on TV. "You ain't seen nothing yet, darling." In the bedroom she unbuttoned her blouse to reveal a red, lacy bra.

"I... I feel like we're rushing things here." George looked forlorn, a glass of untouched scotch in one hand and the bottle in the other.

Kelly removed the glass and bottle from his hands, setting them on the bedside table. "It's a small window of opportunity, George." She tugged his belt loose.

"Aren't we a little old?"

"I had a dream last night." She reached under his shirt and gently dragged her nails across his chest. "I was holding a baby." Of their own volition his nipples hardened. "I believe God wants us to have a baby."

Panic was hammering in George's chest. "God?"

"Otherwise, what's the point of being married?" Her lips moved lightly up his neck.

"Well, yes." George, relenting, leaned his neck into Kelly's mouth. "But we have been companions on a spiritual journey."

Kelly pulled George's shirt over his head and pressed her bra, her breasts into his bare chest. She stuck her hand into her underwear and pulled out a slick finger and dragged it along his lips, "Feel how wet I am?"

George, astounded, jumped back.

"Too much?" Kelly asked.

"A bit."

She slumped back on the bed. "I don't even know how to go about this anymore."

George grabbed his scotch and threw the drink back in one toss, then poured a healthy two ounces. "You're certain about this?"

"I would like a child." Kelly corrected herself. "I would like us to have a child."

George sat down beside Kelly. "I have to tell you something first." He took a large swallow from his scotch. "You're not going to like it."

Kelly stared at him. Silent.

"I have a problem."

Kelly pushed her palms against her eyes. "Jesus, George."

He rushed on. "There's only one way for me to get a, you know," George waved his hand, "erection." He didn't add *with a woman*.

Kelly waited, sipped her scotch and kept her eyes on George.

"When we perform—" George began, "—and you sing. I have to say I'm extremely grateful to be sitting down at the organ. Because, you know," George waved his hand again, "my organ is listening too." George stared at the ground, his cheeks burning. "Not so much at weddings, pop music doesn't have the same effect, but when I hear you sing at a funeral and I see you reaching out to those mourners," he shook his head, "I'm sorry but I can't help myself."

"You get a hard—an erection, when I sing?"

"Only when you sing hymns." He took a deep

breath then he whispered. "I'm good you know. I'm good with the way things are."

"Me too, George. I'm just worried about what comes after us. Are we the end of it? Are you and I the end of the line?"

"We could always adopt."

"That would take years. I know it's selfish but I want a child that comes from me. From *us*. My body is ready, George. Right now. Tonight."

George understood that a no would mean the end of them. He understood there were worse things than sexual union between a man and his wife. George hadn't thought of Brian since their honeymoon and if it meant saving his marriage—he nodded. "Okay." George closed his eyes, "Let's do it."

He barely had the words out when Kelly's hands were at his zipper, expertly removing his pants and underwear. When George dared to open his eyes she was leaning over him dressed only in her scarlet bra. "Would you like me to sing?"

George nodded.

Kelly kissed George, slowly moving down his stomach with her lips. When she reached the top of his pubic hair she lifted her head, began to tickle his balls lightly with her fingernails and began. "Ave Maria." She enunciated each syllable, holding the notes impossibly long as the words floated over George's head. He felt her hot breath warm the top of his pubic bone and groaned softly.

"Gratia plena," she sang. George's penis rose toward her voice.

Excitement surged through Kelly's gut. "Dominus tecum," and her hand moved up and down his shaft.

"Benedicta tu in mulieribus."

George, submitted himself to the pleasure of Kelly's hand. And her singing. All points in his body flowed toward his groin.

"Et benedictus fructus ventris tuis Jesu." As Kelly sang, George moved onto his knees and grabbed her from behind, "Sancta Maria." He pressed up against her back pulled her hips down and thrust himself into her. Surprised, Kelly pushed back against her husband.

She gasped with pleasure and her voice wavered slightly, "Sancta Maria."

George's heavy breathing in her ear made her nipples spring to life and push against her bra. She reached toward her clit.

They made it through the rest of "Ave Maria," "Holy God We Praise Thy Name" and the first verse and chorus of "You Raise me Up" before George shuddered and gasped and Kelly, pushing back hard against her husband's increasing limpness, came in a tight little shudder too.

Kelly turned to face George. "That wasn't so bad."

He kissed her deeply, exhilarated by her performance. And his.

Then Kelly started to laugh. "I swear, George, I was just waiting for you to tell me you were gay."

*

5

GEORGE PULLS THE CAR INTO THE CHURCH parking lot. "Hey little momma," he shakes Kelly, "we've arrived."

Kelly opens her eyes against the late morning sun. A white hearse is parked in front of Holy Cross Church. Two limousines pull up and mourners, chatting quietly, exit the vehicle. Kelly counts twelve; they cluster on the steps while three more sedans deposit another nine family members.

"Look at them all," Kelly says.

George nods. "You'll knock them dead." George always utters some version of knock them dead before a funeral. It's his kind of funny and, at this point in their relationship, Kelly thinks it's funny too.

Kelly lets her head fall back against the seat rest. "I guess Shane is never going to speak to me again."

"You'll just have to keep reaching out."

"He called me a sanctimonious bitch."

George takes her hand. "Would you like me to call him?"

"Are you out of your mind?" Kelly snaps. Then she sighs, "I'm sorry."

"What time is Shirley's service?"

Kelly closes her eyes "Ten."

"Well, maybe you should call Shane when we get home."

"Maybe."

Kelly remains with her eyes closed. She brushes an obstinate tear from the corner of her eye. There will be no more midnight calls from Shirley, no more embarrassing gestures of friendship. There will be no more remorse. Now it is over. Kelly runs her hand over her widening stomach that just this morning fluttered with life, or she had gas. It's a little too early in the pregnancy to know the difference.

George sighs, "We shouldn't have taken this job."

"Don't be silly. I wouldn't have gone back anyway. And you know I love to sing for you." Kelly opens the car door and swings her legs out. "Come on darling, let's go make some people cry."

REGINA

I WASN'T IN LOVE WITH THE KLEPTOMANIAC but he was a good dresser. He had the look of a fag, or maybe a Christian. He didn't do poppers but he liked gay bars. When we went to the Jackson Victory tour we each swallowed a 20/20, a pink heart and a black baby then gritted our teeth from the back row of BC Place while mothers and their seven-year-old daughters did the wave. Michael Jackson was about five miles away, a little Muppet doing the moonwalk.

Bobby preferred words like "purloin" and "pocket" to steal. Items he pocketed included a General Electric iron and a gold Braun coffee filter. He told me stories of his thievery without emotion. I asked, "Doesn't it bother you to take part in something so morally questionable?" But he said it wasn't immoral to steal from Eatons and I supposed he had a point. He was into business plans. I was into being a movie star or a lesbian. It wasn't as easy a choice as it might sound.

I was twenty-three years old. I watched *Personal Best* pretty much weekly. I was no jock but the sight of Muriel Hemingway and Patrice Donnelly running up the sand dunes brought a small jolt to my belly. It's not that I hadn't tried my hand at sports—in grade nine I had played on the school field hockey team. But what I remembered was a huge lump on my shin from the fucking ball smashing into me, and going to the coach's house for a year-end party. The coach's roommate was an amateur photographer. She shot close-ups of flowers and I especially liked the violets but when we left, Janet Barnes, a tenth grader with a line-up of male admirers, said "Dykes." Like she was spitting. I didn't say a word.

I was working at the Blue Sky Hotel, dropping speed and serving beer in its renamed, and newly renovated, pub, High Jinks. The bar was designed to attract the young upwardly mobile crowd and EXPO visitors. But despite the hotel's efforts, High Jinks still had daytime regulars with names like Al and Fred and Jack. My name was Dear or Darling. They were veterans or roofers or they sold tires. I wasn't really certain because I never asked but that's how the cheap bastards struck me. They held up one or two fingers— usually two—to indicate how many half-pints they'd begin with, offering accidental gestures of peace.

The management at the Blue Sky Hotel wanted to put a stop to the old hangers-on from the hotel's terry-cloth tabletop era, which had ended about three months before, but the Blue Sky was the last refuge of men like Al and Fred and Jack, surrounded as they were by Robson Street's new yuppies, designer boutiques and gay men. Fred and Al and Jack tried to be pleasant but the future was encroaching and it didn't like their yellow fingers and dingy suits. They were not accustomed to being met with such open distaste. Not that they were finicky but being phased out does not bring out the best in people. They worried about catching AIDS from the bar glasses, smoked endlessly, and failed to tip me.

Each morning the day shift began whether I wanted it to or not. There were forks, knives and spoons to be rolled into burgundy or white napkins, salt and pepper shakers to be wiped down, and ketchup bottles to be refilled.

Most mornings, Derek, the bartender, a pain in the ass on a good day, shimmied past me in the narrow galley designated for prep work and pushed his dick into my rear as though it was an unavoidable collision caused by the tight space.

"Oopsy daisy," he said.

"Did you drop something?" I asked. As if I was going to let the dickhead know I felt anything. I was hoping to instill in Derek the feeling that his pecker was small. Very, very small.

Bobby liked to visit me at work; I didn't kid myself that it was out of affection. He liked the bar's modern renovation, but felt it was wasted on its daytime audience. He especially liked the rows of half-pint glasses that lined its shelves and he was stealing a collection for his small kitchen.

Derek, who admired Bobby's bold thievery, would call him over. "Hey kid!" he'd pat the bar, indicating that Bobby should sit down. He'd place a bowl of soup and a coffee in front of Bobby and say, "Don't worry Bob, it's on the house."

"Thanks, Derek!" Free soup was a source of great pleasure to Bobby, especially on Friday when the Blue Sky Hotel served Manhattan clam chowder as opposed to the creamy New England version.

When Derek went to pick up food orders in the kitchen Bobby would pull an airplane bottle of brandy out of his pocket and dump its contents into his coffee. Derek was under the impression that Bobby didn't imbibe alcohol, as Bobby didn't like to pay for expensive drinks in bars.

The management at High Jinks installed a state of the art television screen that lit up the back wall behind the dance floor and broadcast Much Music, which had been launched just before the bar's renovation. There was an endless rotation of Wham!, Tears for Fears and Whitney Houston singing sugary pop music, and despite my contempt for the top 40 I caught myself singing: I found out what I've been missing, always on the run. I've been looking for someone. I knew the whole damn song.

My plan was to work at High Jinks until I got my first big acting break. I had finally landed the role of Sleeping

Woman in Wheelchair, keeping in mind there were no small parts, only small actors. The play *Liebchen, No Matter What the Future Brings*, a one-act show starring a voluptuous femme named Margot, was written by an unusually tall fag named Harlow. In the play Margot went on about the movie *Casablanca* and how she wished she had been born a hermaphrodite. Margot played the parts of Rick, Ilsa and Lazlo; Harlow played the roles of Sam and Captain Renault. The way I understood it, Sleeping Woman in Wheelchair was meant to act as a metaphor for straight chicks still crippled by their attachment to the patriarchal status quo.

It was a strange play attended by even stranger people. I only had one line in the play, delivered just before the final curtain, when I reared my head and called "Of all the gin joints in all the towns in all the world, she walks into mine." Then I let my head drop down again and feigned sleep. Harlow was very interested in the homosexual subtext of *Casablanca*. I was interested in seeing who came to the play and would try to guess through my lowered lashes what the people in the front row were wearing. I could only speculate on their attire based on their choice of shoes and my delight in my accurate guesses lent a kind of veracity to the delivery of my line.

Still, I was left with some serious doubts about my choice of careers. Harlow was one of those freaky smart guys, the kind with no social skills. He was a conspiracy theorist who could make you believe the timing of the lights on Granville was the result of evil minds at work. So his play was not the sort of production that anyone looking for the next Heather Locklear was going to attend. Also, I was scared shitless the play would be reviewed in *The Province* and my parents would discover that I was hanging out with freaky homos and disrespecting *Casablanca*. My parents' first date was at a drive-in screening of the movie and they revered Humphrey Bogart. There was no danger of anyone from *The Province* showing up, but the worry consumed me. Finally, I hated theatre spaces; their dark back stages filled me with anxiety. But I had already written in my high-school yearbook that I was going to take Hollywood by storm and I had no idea how to back out of such an outlandish promise.

A FEW MONTHS AFTER I STARTED working at High Jinks, and right after the end of the run of *Liebchen, No Matter What the Future Brings*, I ran into a girl I knew from high school. We had been fiercely close for about three months one spring when boys first started driving cars. We were fifteen and charmed our way into backseats for off-campus lunches at Tastee Burger, where we would share deep fried mushrooms. Drama always surrounded Susan; she had an air of mystery. She would disappear for an hour or maybe a day and reappear with her boyfriend. It seemed like they were always fighting. I kept waiting for her to confide in me but she never did.

Susan stepped in front of me on Denman Street—
she materialized, like she had been transported from the
back of a Ford Bronco eight years before. Except now
her hair was springing with dreadlocks. If I could have
talked I would have said "Of all the gin joints..."

"Hey," she said. She stepped in to hug me, a musky
aroma of garlic and Dr. Bonner's peppermint soap
rose from her arms. She had a kid with her, a boy she'd
named Cedar. Now she called herself Starr. She stood
toe to toe with me. I wanted to step back a few inches
but didn't want to come across as hung up. Cedar
clutched her leg. Someone had drawn a yellow daisy on
his cheek with markers.

"Nice." I pointed to the flower.

"Cedar loves flowers." Starr told me.

Cedar was silent on the issue.

She asked me if I wanted to smoke a joint so we
headed toward the beach. She told me she had been dat-
ing a real estate agent friend of her father's when she got
pregnant. She wasn't sure if he was the dad or if it was a
random tree planter that she'd picked up at The Smilin'
Buddha one Friday night when the realtor had to go to
some charity event with his wife. I looked back at Cedar
who was trailing behind us. "I don't believe in hiding,
the truth from kids," Starr said. "He also knows there's
no Santa Claus, no Easter Bunny, et cetera."

When Cedar got tired Starr carried him on her
shoulders. The only word the kid said was "Up" and
she lifted him without comment. His fingers were soft

looking and streaked with dirt. He gripped her dreads like reins. I made clicking sounds with my tongue and pretended to ride a horse beside him. Cedar just looked at me. Starr told me he was an old soul.

After we smoked the joint we leaned against a sun bleached log and watched Cedar poke his toe in the water—over and over he stuck the big toe of his right foot into the Pacific. He stood there doing that while Starr told me about her romance with our grade ten English teacher, Mr. Heaton. Susan's supposed boyfriend, Allan Dickinson, was doing the biology teacher, Ms. James, and the four of them double dated all through grade eleven and twelve. But Susan left a devastated Mr. Heaton behind and came to the city where she connected with the real estate agent, made a baby and became Starr.

Then Starr told me her parents, the lawyer and the lovely housewife who still held hands after all these years, were getting a divorce. Her mom had discovered her dad was keeping a secret love-nest apartment for daytime assignations with assistants and call girls. Starr said she figured it was about time her mother became self-actualized. The role of lawyer's wife had sucked the joy out of Starr's mother and all that was left was a thin middle-aged woman with blonde highlights and a husband who couldn't keep his pants zipped. Then she started to cry. She was wracked with tears, snot leaking out of her nose and spit pulling between her lips. Cedar sat down in the water.

I told her I was going to be late for work and stood up to leave. She insisted I give her my number and so, with perfect delivery, I made one up and told her to call me. When I hugged her she held onto me, breathing deeply the way hippies like to hug—like we were both really in the moment.

"Mmmm," she said. Then she gave me a long and thoughtful look, "We were meant to connect today."

I waved at Cedar and hurried up the beach away from Starr, who used to be Susan, thinking about how, if I meant to avoid her, I'd have to stay away from health food stores and Granville Island.

A FEW WEEKS AFTER I DITCHED STARR on English Bay, Bobby got us free tickets to go hear Dr. Helen Caldicott talk about *Nuclear Madness*. Bobby never said no to free things. I wasn't into politics but Bobby had come into some weed and he was willing to share so I tagged along. A word to the wise: don't get high before you go to some lecture on the nuclear threat.

Dr. Helen Caldicott brought up a slide that showed a clock; it was three minutes to midnight. Americans were all jacked up on Ronald Reagan, whose Strategic Defense Initiative included some kind of see-through shield over the USA. Of course she articulated it better, and with a nice Australian accent, but what I heard was, we were as good as fucked and it was no help for me to think that each one of us could do something to bring some portion of misery to an end because what difference would a difference make?

Bobby had smuggled a mickey of Southern Comfort into the lecture. I wasn't a big drinker then, but I was looking for anything that would tame the anxiety that was sucking the air out of my lungs.

"Hey, slow down on that," Bobby whispered.

"I'll buy you some drinks later," I replied. That shut him up. By the time the lecture ended I was a mess because the world was a mess and it was three minutes to fucking midnight. Bobby, on the other hand, hardly noticed.

"I love Australian accents," he said. "They're so charming." Bobby popped a piece of Trident in his mouth. "Want to go to the Gandy Dancer?"

"If they'll let me in."

"They will if you're with me."

"Do you think it seems kind of shallow to go dancing after that lecture?"

"What else are you going to do?" he asked. He had a point.

By the time we left the club I was hammered. I suggested to Bobby that we go back to his place for a little shag.

"Why?" he asked.

"Why not?" I said.

Bobby would take anything that wasn't offered to him but insisted upon negotiating this.

"Bobby, if you're gay you don't have to hide it from me."

"I'm not!" he squealed, "I swear on my mother's life."

Bobby didn't even like his parents.

After a short negotiation Bobby agreed it would be a good idea, fun even, to have sex. We shook hands on it and walked back to his place.

The next morning my dread was exacerbated by a terrific hang-over. My head was beating its own rhythm that had nothing to do with the rest of my body and I was surrounded by a halo of regret. When I walked into High Jinks, Tears for Fears were blasting from the wall of video. "Welcome to your life," they sang. "There's no turning back."

Later, when the old men arrived for lunch, Fred said, "You're quiet."

"I'm not feeling well."

Al or Jack, I could never tell them apart, choked on his cigarette and coughed out the smoke while his buddy clapped his back. "Oh, I know all about that," he said. The three old sleazebags giggled.

I expected he knew fuck-all but I smiled, "You have the flu?"

"Every morning, darling. Every bloody morning."

Frank, who had radar for my weakness, patted my ass in what I imagine he thought a parental fashion and asked, "Did you get lucky last night, dear?"

A jet of anger tore across my eyes and I nearly dropped my full tray on their table. I should have poured a drink on the dirty old bastard but, instead, I left their filthy ashtray untouched. Not that they noticed, they were the kind of smokers who let their ashes fall onto their suit jackets and pants.

"No," I told Fred. I left them without taking a drink order.

I wanted to crawl into the back corner of the stock room, behind the maraschino cherries and paper towels, and sleep. I wished I were already old. I wished I'd already lived my life and had kids and a husband I hardly talked to. I wished I had adoring fans and I wished it wouldn't bother me so much that we were going to blow ourselves to smithereens. It was such bad luck to be born in the nuclear age.

I DON'T KNOW WHY I WAS SURPRISED when Bobby showed up for lunch; he was a creature of habit and he loved his free soup. But when he walked through the door it occurred to me that he might be a socio-path, or a moron. That morning I had left him sleeping and headed north across the Burrard Street Bridge just as the city woke up for breakfast. I assumed he would have understood by my exit that I needed a bit of space. Seeing Bobby brought to mind my mother's favourite saying: *When you assume you make an ass out of u and me.* Maybe Bobby thought we were going to become an item. Or maybe it was just a guy thing.

Bobby called me over to the bar. "I had a great time," he said.

"Me too." Theatre school, I was thinking, was pay-ing off in ways I'd never imagined. In fact, I had found the whole thing to be pretty boring. Bobby's pet rat Andy, who was allowed to wander around his little bachelor apartment, had distracted me. Bobby loved that rat and did nothing until it jumped on the bed for the third time. Then he got up and put the rat in its cage. I stood there looking at Bobby, thinking of what I really wanted to say and I was working up to it, but shit always happens when you're hung-over.

"Hi there," I heard fucking Starr say. I turned to look at her and so did Bobby. "Your number's out of service." She shrugged and held her hands in front of her like she was giving up.

I think there is something you're supposed to do in these situations but I just said, "I've got customers." And I walked away. I saw Starr climb onto the stool beside Bobby; I could only guess at the level of his contempt, which was certain to be great. I was going to have to tell her I gave her my old number; that I was mixed up because I was stoned. I was going to have to give her my real number. My mouth was dry and tasted sour.

What was Starr's deal? Why would she even want to see me? And why the fuck did I tell her where I worked? That's the thing with Starr, you just told her things you didn't mean to. When she was Susan it was just the same. I was in love with her then. She was beautiful and puzzling. She would stare deep into my eyes. I thought she knew something I didn't, and I loved her even more for that. Now she was probably talking some crap about karma to Bobby, who was going to harass me about her for weeks just because I screwed him once. I was thinking I should get out of this city, go back to school and study Broadcast Journalism.

The video soundtrack of my day had segued to George Michael whining "Should've known better than to cheat a friend." It was hard not to think he was speaking directly to me, even if I had to substitute the word screw for cheat. I was buried in stupid shit. Starr was insane, Bobby was a prick and I was invisible, terrified of auditions, and now also panicked by the thought of the red button that would send missiles raining down on waitresses, thieves, hippies and stupid fucking drunks. And a port city like Vancouver was sure to be targeted.

Two gay men walked past the window. They were dressed in tight, white tank tops, jeans and spiky belts. Their hair fell into their eyes and they both wore Fluevogs. The guy closest to the window saw something on the sidewalk, stopped, and let out a little squeal. Then the two of them began to shriek with laughter and they walked away. They seemed to be so okay with standing out and all of that stuff.

"Faggots," Fred said.

"Don't worry, they'll be dead soon," one of his cronies added. And the three of them laughed. But those gay boys were gone from the window, oblivious to the rancour of the old men.

"Darling," Fred called, "bring us another round."

I know those old farts figured they were better than me and it made me shiver with anger but I got them their beer.

I'd had it up to here with drunks. Bobby was just a well-dressed thief, and the person closest to him was a jealous rat. Hippies were totally out of style but Starr was too far gone to notice. I watched the two of them talking at the bar, Starr placed her hand over top of Bobby's heart and he shot me a look. I flashed my teeth like a smile at him and Starr turned around and waved. I smiled at Starr too, what else was I going to do? Anyway, tomorrow was payday, and, Liebchen, no matter what the future was bringing, I was going to buy a Greyhound ticket to take me as far from the west coast as possible, which would probably be some hick town like Regina. Don't think the joke was lost on me.

VALERIE'S BUSH

IN THE COMMUNAL SHOWER of the hot yoga studio there were two women as bald as Barbie dolls. Another woman, who Val made to be at least five years older than she was, sported only a little triangle of hair on her pubic bone, her long labia hung below. The blonde woman showering immediately to her right wore a straight rectangle down the centre of her pubis.

Aside from a careful clipping close to her vaginal entry, because that's just good manners, Valerie's genitals were covered in a large, curly bush of hair. It had been almost twenty years since her pussy had been on the market, almost twenty years since she'd had to consider its attractiveness to strangers. In that time the natural look had fallen out of fashion, which Valerie was media savvy enough to know, but not alert enough to realize might affect a woman her age.

THE SALON RECEPTIONIST DIRECTED VALERIE to a small studio near the back of the store. Peaceful sounds of piano and waterfalls were being piped into the room, lavender and sweet grass hung in the air. "Take off your pants and undies and place the sheet over your lap," the receptionist said happily. "Oh, and the candles are soy." She smiled, dimmed the lights and closed the door behind her.

Then the esthetician entered the room. Her blonde hair was pulled into a neat ponytail, the tips of her bangs a bright pink that matched the non-latex gloves she pulled on with a snap. She wore a white lab coat unbuttoned to reveal a firm, muscular body and surprisingly large knockers. *Live, Laugh, Love* was tattooed in script across her collarbone. Val reflexively touched her salt and pepper hair, which was cut short, a practical style suited to an urban farmer or nun. Vanity belonged to a paradigm Valerie rejected, but the lean esthetician, in her low-slung jeans and flat belly, made Val feel dried up, dull, and chubby. The esthetician stretched her arms over her head, a tattooed branch of cherry blossoms bloomed up her abdomen. She stepped toward Val.

"Oh!" she exclaimed when she drew back the sheet to reveal Valerie's hirsute mound. She dropped onto her stool, perplexed.

Valerie stared at the ceiling. "It's my first time," she muttered.

"You know, I've been working here for ten years now and this is a first for me. That's *a lot* of hair. No one lets it get out of hand any more. Not even the hippies. Jeez." She sighed, "I'm going to have to start

with scissors." As she stood over Valerie with scissors
in hand she said, "It's very important that you lie perfectly still. I wouldn't want to cut you."

"Okay."

"So what brought you in?" Ingrid asked. Now that she
was closer, Valerie could read her name tag. It occurred to
Valerie that it was rude of Ingrid not to introduce herself,
but maybe it was the shock of pubic hair that silenced her.

"I thought it was time to switch things up," Valerie
answered.

"Spice up the old relationship?"

"That's over." Valerie tried not to have any inflec-
tion but her voice rose sharply as she pronounced the
end of her relationship.

"Oh, I'm sorry." Ingrid consoled her, "Trust me, I
know break-ups can be rough. Any kids?"

Valerie shook her head.

"Well that's for best, I suppose."

"We didn't want kids," Valerie said. "Except now
she's with someone who's twelve years younger and
they're having a baby."

"That's just cold," Ingrid said. "Now, what is it
you're thinking of doing here?" She asked pointing to
Valerie's trimmed bush.

"I hadn't really thought about it," Valerie confessed.

"How do you even know they're having a baby?"
Ingrid asked.

Valerie turned her head toward the wall, blushing
at the thought of her last meeting with Margot. Val had

mistaken Margot's nervous call for remorse. She had imagined a reconciliation was about to be proposed. She dropped everything, which was, in fact, nothing, and raced out to meet Margot.

"Hey," Margot said when Val sat down. "I've only got twenty-five minutes until Sue picks me up."

Val, doing her best to keep her face blank, nodded. "Sure. I'm up to my ears in work myself."

"Oh good," Margot said. "I won't keep you." She lifted her coffee to her lips and eyed Valerie. "You look a little tired," she said.

"I stayed out too late last night," Val answered. "Partying."

"I have to tell you something," Margot began. "And I don't know how to start so I'm just going to say it in a rush and then we can process it from there. Okay?"

"Sure."

"Sue is pregnant. And we're getting married."

Valerie swallowed. "Making an honest women of her, I guess?"

Margot laughed. "I know it sounds crazy, but I'm happy and I just wanted you to know."

"Why?"

"Well, it's a small community. Gossip and such."

Valerie nodded.

"Is there anything you'd like to say to me?" Margot asked.

"Is there anything you'd like me to say?"

"I hate it when you do that!"

"Do what?" Valerie asked.

"Turn shit around. I'm just trying to be honest here."

"I appreciate your honesty." Valerie stood up.

"Don't go," Margot said.

But Valerie had no intention of making small talk with her formally opposed to marriage—same-sex or otherwise—ex-partner when she could be home watching reruns of *Criminal Minds*.

"THEY WANTED ME TO KNOW FIRST," Valerie told Ingrid. "They didn't want me to hear it through the grapevine."

"What a crock of shit!" Ingrid said. Then she perched her hands on her hips and suggested, "You know, dear, I think we should just take it all off."

"Isn't it kind of weird for a woman my age?"

"Not at all. And while those bitches are up all night with a colicky baby, God willing, you'll be getting your groovy on with a brand spanking new vajayjay. You won't regret it."

Valerie decided to be daring, "I guess there's no harm in trying."

"That's the spirit! You know, a lot of lesbians come in here."

"They do?"

"You bet. At first I was surprised. I thought you girls wouldn't mind hair down there, but then later I thought why would you like hair down there, any more than a guy, say?" As she spoke she laid thin strips of wax-covered fabric across Valerie's bush.

"I think we do it because it's in fashion," Valerie said. "And, I think it's in fashion because pornography is so pervasive in our culture."

"True that," Ingrid laughed. "Now, this is going to sting a little."

The pain of a thousand infinitesimal perforations was ripped from Val. A tear rolled down the side of her face.

"That's the worst of it," Ingrid promised. "But you might see a little bruising. Like I said, there was *a lot* of hair." She tore the next strip.

Valerie gasped at the pain, which hadn't lessened, not at all.

"Think of it as your break-up haircut," Ingrid suggested.

CYCLING BACK TO HER NEW APARTMENT she felt a definite lack beneath her clothing. Her cotton panties rubbed against the flesh that had been unexposed since Valerie was thirteen. It was out of character for her to behave so impulsively, and all over a gift certificate to a hot yoga studio. She pedaled hard, enjoying the wind against her face. Although she worried that her pubic hair might have served an important biological function, Valerie felt liberated by its removal. She was unfettered and that was just fine, for once. Val let her bike coast down a small hill; it was time to say something to Margot, to wish her luck, to let her go.

Valerie had just the thing to say goodbye.

That evening, in the shadow of dusk, from across the street, Val watched the house that she once shared with Margot. A light burned in the kitchen; surely they were back there. Valerie pulled her bottom lip between her teeth as she considered the intimacy the single light suggested. She cradled a large stone in her palm, a black rock she had picked from the beach when she and Margot had taken their first vacation together along the Oregon coast. They had been so in love they barely had time to pitch their tent before they were back inside it, fucking.

The rock was divided in half by a perfect white line and promised its possessor good luck. Valerie had been ecstatic when she found it, harbinger that it was of all the good that was yet to come. It was a big rock, almost five inches long and one inch thick. It was unusually lucky. When they returned from their trip Val set the stone carefully on her dresser and loved it all these years. She held it now to her cheek, as a way of saying goodbye. Then, she pitched the rock through Margot's front window and sprinted down the alley toward her bike.

BACK IN HER APARTMENT, CAREFULLY and without regret, Valerie considered herself in the mirror. The blue curve of a bruise was tucked into the crease of her thigh where hours before coarse black hair had flourished. She would have to avoid the yoga studio until the mark faded. She might have been a dupe. She might have missed the signals of Margot's affair, of her leaving, but Valerie wasn't such an idiot that she couldn't change with the times. She traced her fingers over her depilated flesh, smooth as woman's face, enjoying her new reflection.

CANARY

JUDI KNOWS YOU ONLY GET ONE SHOT at a first impression so she won't take no for an answer. Kyle, cheeks burning, pulls a pillow close to his chest, hugs his knees. Judi has ripped off her shirt and dropped it on the floor. Her bra is pink and made to hold volume. He tries not to look but his eyes are drawn to the rosy lace and long line of cleavage. Judi slaps the flesh that falls over the top of her jeans. "Maybe I just need to wear something that draws attention upward to my breasts?" Kyle shrugs but Judi isn't looking. "Kyle?" Silence. "Kyle!"

"I said I don't know," he mutters. He chews on the denim at his knee.

"Well, speak up so I can hear you," she snaps.

"Can I leave now?"

"Do I look finished to you?"

Kyle sighs and lets his head fall back against the wall. "It's my date."

"And you don't want to spend all night on public transit." Judi pulls a black V-neck decorated with glittery flowers over her head. "What's her name?"

"Rose."

"I think I can make this work." She surveys herself in the mirror. "Rose. That's a pretty name. What colour is her hair?"

"Black."

"Was she born here?"

"Her parents are from the Philippines. If that's what you're asking."

"I'll wear my chunky silver don't you think?" Judi leans over Kyle and breathes in deeply near his armpits, "And you should take a shower."

JUDI IS SIPPING HOT WATER and lemon but can't stop thinking about the Honey Nut Cheerios in the cupboard. She stacks the newspaper on the recycling pile. That guy in North Korea is the bee's knees. No, she thinks, he takes the cake. And now with Kyle going out on a proper date, Judi blows out a gust of anxiety, she never should have read that damn paper. Anyway, a few Honey Nut Cheerios beats the hell out of a bag of potato chips. Judi grabs a handful from the box and sucks them into her mouth. For God's sake she doesn't care where that girl Rose comes from, although it's a fact that mixed race babies are so much cuter than the rest. "Kyle!" she calls, "Do you want me to buy you some condoms?"

In his room, Kyle flops onto his bed, electrified with remorse. What possessed him to tell her anything about this? Judi knocks on his door. "Sweetheart?"

"Please don't talk about this." He speaks in a low, even tone.

She opens the door and pops her head into his room. "I could put condoms in the bathroom and fill them up when they're empty. No questions."

"Don't do that."

"I just want you to be safe."

Kyle stares at the ceiling of his room, dumb with misery.

"Darling, I would advise you not to be so hung up." Judi closes the door while Kyle tries to imagine his ceiling is the ocean and he is alone on an island and he knows what to eat to stay alive and there is a waterfall he can bathe in.

ROSE'S FATHER SHAKES KYLE'S HAND and waves to Judi from the front door. Judi reaches her arm out the car window and wiggles her fingers toward the porch. She calls hello in her good neighbour voice. Judi believes a little bit of pleasant goes a long way. The girl, Rose, in her tight jeans and high heels, reminds Judi of her own teenaged self who loved the Bee Gees and could dance the Hustle. Well, Judi was taller, and she had a bigger rack and light brown hair, permed like Barbara Streisand when she sang "Guilty" with Barry Gibb, but it's more a feeling than a look anyway.

The kids don't speak as they move down the walk toward the car. Kyle looks positively depressed; maybe he's homosexual. Why wouldn't he think he could come out to her? Kyle opens the door and jumps into the car; Rose follows after him. "Kyle!" Judi's voice is shrill, "I can't believe what I just witnessed." Rose and Kyle share an anxious look; they didn't even touch on the sidewalk.

"What?" Kyle asks.

"Ladies first, Kyle. Hold the door open for the girl, for pity's sake."

He shoots an abashed look toward Rose, "Sorry."

"It's okay." She smiles at Kyle, then at Judi. "Really Mrs. Mercer. I didn't even notice."

"Call me Judi. Mrs. Mercer is my mother." Kyle looks out the window. His mother is already at it, even after she promised not to talk.

Judi activates the door locks because you never know and stranger things have happened, and she is a woman alone in a car with two fourteen-year-olds, and that can look pretty vulnerable to the unsavory sorts who wait at intersections looking for cars to jack. Of course Judi knows there's not an abundance of these people, but one is all you need, right? Case in point, that guy in West Virginia. Life can throw all sorts of curve balls at you.

"First stop is Bean There?" Judi knows the kids are going for coffee first but Kyle is just sitting there and she doesn't feel right with all the silence in the car.

"Yeah." Kyle has only told her that eight thousand times.

"Are you a coffee drinker, Rose?" Judi opens the floor to conversation.

"For sure." Rose is enthusiastic.

"You're a little young, though, aren't you?"

"Pardon me?"

"Coffee. It stunts your growth, doesn't it?"

"Uh-"

Kyle offers, "Rose is already taller than her mom."

"Well, that's probably the growth hormones in milk."

Kyle wants to open the door and roll out of the car like James Bond.

"Oh, don't get me started, Rose. I have an opinion on everything."

"Okay." Rose looks at Kyle; he mouths the word sorry, holds his hands up like Jesus in front of the mob.

"What's your favourite subject, dear?"

Rose isn't sure if the question is for her or Kyle. She waits for Kyle, but he is silent. "P.E.?"

"You like to run around then?"

"I like chemistry, too," Rose adds.

"That came out wrong," says Judi.

"What?" Rose is flustered.

"I didn't mean to imply you're slutty."

Kyle feels hysterical. He starts to laugh and softly bang his head on Rose's shoulder. Rose let's free a small laugh.

*

THE BARISTA DROPS TWO BROWN MUGS in front of Kyle and Rose. Each mug is topped with three inches of chocolate whipped cream. From her seat at the counter Judi tries not to look like she is spying, but those coffees are more desserts than drinks. You could buy lunch at McDonalds for the price of one of those beverages. When she was young her friends pulled her out of bed in her pajamas and took her to McDonalds for breakfast. It was her sixteenth birthday. Now, these kids wouldn't be caught dead in a McDonalds. Not that that's a bad thing. Judi sips her Americano, we're turning into a bunch of fatties and McDonalds can't offer enough apple slices to fix that.

Judi envies those kids with their expectations and dreams. They haven't a bloody clue. Sometimes she thinks she should just sit Kyle down and lay it out to him: Kid, no one on God's green earth (except me) gives a shit about you. Just as a way of preparing him for what's ahead. We're all so forgettable, she wants to tell him. Billions (at the very least) of people have died and are lost to time already. She doesn't want him to get his hopes up.

Of course, she doesn't want him to kill himself either, and Rose is a promising beginning. That girl's got hips on her and a little waist that goes in like a Barbie Doll. No boobs to speak of. It'll be curious to see how far they go. Judi jumps up, "Chop, chop!" she calls across the crowded café. Rose and Kyle look up, startled and excruciated by her antics. Judi taps her wrist to indicate time. "They're not going to hold the movie for us!"

THE KIDS ARE WATCHING A SING-ALONG screening of *The Sound of Music*. Judi can't decide if that's gay or just funny. She and Kyle have watched the movie now and then as it makes its annual rounds on TV, but Rose's family make a ritual of it. Every Easter they gather around the television with chocolates and popcorn and watch the marvellous tale of love and escape. They must be Catholics. *Marvellous tale of love and escape*, those are Rose's words, clearly her parents have coached her. Judi believes in a more hands-off approach.

She digs through her bag for her novel. This year Judi is getting through the classics. That Heathcliff was a piece of work. How did a stuffy, English virgin ever come up with the likes of him? Next on her list is the entire Jane Austen series, starting with *Pride and Prejudice*, because the movie was pretty good. Then, on the table to her right, Judi sees Jennifer Aniston on the cover of *People*. Poor little thing. It just goes to show you that money is no guarantee of happiness, although Judi wouldn't mind giving wealth a chance. Tropical resorts and good haircuts must take out the sting of rejection just a little bit.

Judi can't get comfortable in the crappy chairs they've left in the lobby of the cinema. These little independent cinemas all look like they've been furnished with pickings from the dumpster, it sure as hell feels like it. The place is staffed by scruffy university types, one of the boys unfortunate enough to be losing his hair before twenty-five. Still, it wouldn't hurt him to shave.

The two boys behind the counter are having a heated discussion. *Dude!* she hears them call to one another. Something about a political science class because they said the words Canada's parliamentary system. Shouldn't boys that age talk about girls and getting lucky? The puritans have taken over. If those kids had a clue what went on in the discotheques they'd be crying over their spilt milk. Judi blames AIDS because it scares the shit out of everybody. And rightly so, of course.

Judi closes her eyes and lets her youth wash over her. Cel-le-brate good times, she hums, Come on! We're going to have a celebration. The boys were fond of her and she was partial to the boys. Not everyone liked that, certainly not her mother, but Judi was in love with love. Nowadays, it seems, virginity is all the rage. Judi releases a sigh, and despite the discomfort of the theatre's lobby seats, she lets herself drift off into sleep, even though her butt is killing her.

THE AUDIENCE IS MAKING ITS WAY up the aisles of the theatre but Kyle and Rose remain seated, holding hands. Their throats are raw from singing with abandon. "I'm sorry about my mom," Kyle whispers.

"She's not so bad."

"She's a freak," he insists and Rose giggles. She leans over and kisses him quickly on the lips. On the lips! "Maybe next time my dad can drive," Rose offers.

"Does he ever shut up? Shout across crowded public spaces?"

Rose bursts with laughter. "He barely opens his mouth."

"I can hardly wait til next time."

Judi, stopped by Kyle's words, backs quietly up the aisle, her eyes burning with humiliation. Too agitated to sit, she paces across the lobby waiting for Kyle and Rose to take their sweet time. She'd like to give them a piece of her mind, but that would just be feeding into Kyle's mean attempt to impress that girl. That's what a boy has to do; he has to distance himself from his mother if he means to get a girl, but to be so unkind!

She watches Kyle and Rose drift toward her. They are no longer holding hands but their faces are bright with excitement. Judi feels her eyes tighten with anger. The smug little shits. They haven't a clue what's coming and she's not about to be their canary in the coalmine. Life is full of poison and soon enough Kyle is going to find that out. He can go live with his father for all she cares because clearly Kyle has fallen victim to his father's toxic attitudes. The bastard.

Rose waves and Judi blasts the kids with a smile. "Ready?" she asks in her lightest tone, "at last?" Kyle nods. Judi turns on her heel and marches out the door,

"Wagons Ho!" she calls. Kyle closes his eyes, bracing himself for the ride home. Rose laces her fingers through his and tugs him toward Judi.

Judi looks toward the back seat, "All set?" Kyle nods and Judi repeats, "All set?" Kyle sighs, "You bet."

If he thinks she's going to give him an inch of satisfaction then he doesn't know her from Adam. Judi presses her foot to the gas; her chest feels like it's closing in on itself; she pushes her thumb and index finger against the bone. Kyle and Rose are too caught up in one another to notice the hard place she is driving toward.

PASSENGER

THE ROAD STRETCHED OUT BEFORE HARVEY, black, faded and lined with cracks. Tracy sat beside him with her arms folded across her chest and a sour look on her face. She had a lot of her mother in her, and no one would ever have charged Ruth with being too soft.

Ruth lost two babies after Tracy. When she had her second miscarriage, the doctors gave Ruth and Harvey no more hope of another pregnancy, but Ruth seemed happy enough after she and Tracy took to Jesus, though Harvey wouldn't have minded a son to shoot the shit with. Sometimes he just grew tired of all these women and their higher moral ground. Like Tracy here, mad as hell at nothing that concerned her.

"Dad," she finally said, "I have to ask you, are you losing your mind? Are you having a breakdown?"

"This may come as a surprise to you Tracy, but I know how to take care of myself."

Tracy sucked her teeth, "Have you even considered what it will be like to drive out there?"

"I'll just stick to the slow lane."

"You have no idea what you're doing."

"Tracy, when's the last time you drove in Toronto?" That shut her up.

"I wonder what you think I do when you're not around," Harvey said softly.

"You know what, dad. I think you should just let me out at the top of the road."

"That'll leave you a two mile walk."

"That's fine," Tracy said. "I need some time to cool down. I have a family expecting a half-way pleasant wife and mother to come home."

"Suit yourself." He steered the truck to the side of the road.

Tracy sighed and pulled her purse tight against her chest. "You remember how to use your phone?"

"I remember how to use my phone."

"And how to check your email and texts?"

"Yes, I do."

She leaned in and hugged him. "Be careful."

"Of course."

"Text me any time you want. I got you a plan with unlimited texting."

"Will do."

"Drive carefully." She opened the door, "And don't forget to text."

"Give my love to the girls. And tell Dale I'll buy him a beer when we get back."

"Daddy, Dale hasn't had a drink in four years."

"Well then, I guess we'll have to give it a pass."

"You could always buy him a coffee."

"Coffee rots your gut."

"Now you're just messing with me."

"Guilty as charged," Harvey said.

Tracy stepped out of the truck and turned back and waved. Harvey pulled slowly away. He could see her in the rear-view mirror, arms crossed and scowling as he drove back toward Rose Prairie Road.

Harvey patted the wooden box on the seat beside him. "Well, Ruthie," he said, "I sure would like a coffee right about now."

Ruth always packed a black and syrupy thermos of coffee for Harvey when he had any amount of driving to do, which had been often enough. Even before he got into sales Harvey had worked as a rig hand and had driven long hours away from the tiny basement apartment they had rented from Irma Vale, whose husband Gord was killed instantly when he had plowed into a semi driving home during a winter storm. Gordon Vale had given sixteen-year-old Harvey his first job, so Irma had a soft spot for Harvey and his quiet, young wife. She'd be dead too, Irma.

Harvey was off the coffee now; even decaf upset his acid reflux. That herbal tea was no better than perfumed water so Harvey went without. "It seems to me Ruthie," he said, "there's a lot of doing without these days." Harvey drank water from a stainless steel jug that Tracy had insisted he used due to plastic bottles being bad for you. It was cumbersome and Harvey felt goofy as hell walking around with the canister, but it made Tracy happy to see him use it, so he did.

BEFORE SHE GOT SO FAT RUTH had been a real looker. She teased her hair up and sprayed it mercilessly, stinking up the entire apartment with Hidden Magic hairspray.

"Jesus Christ, Ruth," he swore. "Are you trying to kill me?"

"Open a window," she said. "You won't be complaining tonight when I have the prettiest hair at the table." She wore a smart pair of brown patent slingbacks and a brown taffeta dress.

"Have you seen the weather out there, ma'am?" Harvey asked. "There's a foot of snow."

"You can carry me in and out of the car."

Harvey laughed and she skipped over and kissed him.

New Year's Eve, 1963.

Tracy was born the following September.

Well, it's all kisses and forgiveness when you're young, isn't it?

STILL, A LITTLE DONUT NEVER HURT NOONE. Harvey was a fritter man; Ruth liked her old fashioned sugar. He pulled into the Tim Horton's parking lot. Roman Wasalyk's granddaughter stood out front smoking a cigarette and giving the trucks at the drive-thru the stink eye. Her hair was cut awfully short for a girl and she was dressed real scruffy. As far as Harvey could tell, university had done nothing for the kid.

He nodded as he walked past, "Rayanne."

She nodded back.

"Beautiful day."

"Yup." She sat down on the edge of a hard red suitcase that lay on its side behind her.

"How are the fritters today?"

"Same as ever, Mr. Hamilton."

"Good to know," he said, and pushed through the door into the donut shop. Rayanne's mother Karen stood behind the counter waiting to take Harvey's order. Rayanne's dad had died in a bar fight in Grande Prairie before his baby was born or his girlfriend was made a wife. Roman Wasalyk took his daughter and granddaughter in, but if you asked Harvey it was just so Roman would have someone to cook and clean for him. He'd never given Karen the time of day when she had been growing up with Tracy.

"Harvey, what can I get for you?" she asked.

"I'll take an apple fritter and an old fashioned sugar for Ruthie."

"We only have old fashioned glazed."

"Well, I guess I'll take an old fashioned glazed." Harvey passed Karen three dollars, "Put the change in the camp box," he said.

"How are you doing, Harvey?" she asked, her voice soft with concern.

"I'm doing good, Karen. How about yourself?"

"Oh, you know. It's up and down."

"I see Rayanne's back."

"Not for long I don't think."

Harvey nodded, "How's your dad?"

"His knees are hurting him."

"That's a pity," Harvey said. "Well, you tell him I said hello."

"That's awfully kind of you, Harvey. He'll be glad to hear that."

Harvey doubted that, but there was no use in saying so.

When he started up the truck, Rayanne was still sitting there chewing on her nails and spitting the bits onto the sidewalk. Harvey pulled up beside her and rolled down his window. "You want a lift?"

"Where are you going?" she said.

"Niagara Falls."

"No shit?"

"Not a word of a lie."

"What's taking you there?"

"I promised Ruth I'd take her there."

"Ruth's in the truck?"

"She is."

Rayanne nodded slowly. "Okay. Do you mind waiting while I tell my mom?"

"Not at all," Harvey said. "Is that your suitcase?"

Rayanne nodded.

"Throw it in the back then." Harvey watched through the plate glass window as Karen placed a hand on her daughter's cheek. He took a bite of his apple fritter. "Well Ruthie, it looks like we've got company."

THE DAMN GIRL DIDN'T OPEN HER MOUTH for nearly eight hours. They were just this side of the Yellowhead when she said "Do you mind if I have a smoke?"

The girl was a fidgeter. Either her fingers were drumming against her thigh, or she was rubbing her feet together, or chewing on the corners of her thumbs. Of course he could have talked, but something perverse rose up in Harvey, he wanted Rayanne to break before he did.

"Fine with me, if you open the window a crack to let the smoke out," he said.

"Great!" Rayanne reached into her pocket and pulled out a pack of smokes; she pushed it open and offered a cigarette to Harvey.

"I gave them up," he said.

Rayanne popped a cigarette into her mouth, lit it and inhaled deeply. "I'm never quitting."

"Never?" Harvey said.

"Nope." Rayanne was firm. "I'm going to die with one of these babies between my lips."

Harvey lifted his eyebrows and nodded, "To each his own."

"Do you miss it?" she asked.

"Smoking?"

Rayanne nodded.

"Not no more."

Rayanne looked out the passenger window.

"I gave it up when the missus caught breast cancer."

Rayanne pointed to the engraved wooden box that rested above the cupholders. "Is that her?"

"Yes ma'am."

"I'm sorry for your loss," she said, then turned again to look out the window.

Harvey bit his lip, he wasn't gonna say nothing if she wasn't, even though he was used to talk. Ruth could talk a blue streak. Her favourite subjects: Jesus, and Harvey's eternal damnation.

"HARVE," RUTH SAID, "surely you realize you are a sinner."

"Damn Ruth, I like to have a drink and I like to have a smoke but if I see a guy walking on the side of the road, I pick him up. If I see a guy needs a coffee or a sandwich, I get him one. I'd give the bugger the coat off my back if he was freezing."

"But you don't believe," she said.

"I believe I should help a guy out if I see he needs it."

"But still, Harvey, you have to accept Jesus," she slapped her chest, "into your heart. Without Him there is no reconciliation with God."

"What about the Jews and the Hindus?"

"I didn't write the Gospel, Harvey. I just follow it."

Harvey stepped toward his wife and kissed her, he pressed hard into her breast. "How about you accept me into your heart and we have a little reconciliation?"

Ruth stepped back and slapped his hand away. "What do you want with a fat old thing like me?"

"Let me show you."

"To what end, Harvey?"

HARVEY'S HANDS TIGHTENED on the steering wheel. Ruth could turn sour on a dime.

"It's true, you know. You can catch breast cancer," Rayanne said.

"What?"

"Well, not like a cold, but you know they're poisoning us."

"They are?"

"They only care about profit."

"Nothing wrong with a little profit."

Rayanne shot Harvey a dangerous look. Kids always think they're the first to notice the world is unkind; it almost made a guy want to laugh.

"How's university treating you?" he asked.

"I'm not going back."

"No?"

"No."

Talking to this girl was like pulling teeth. "Why not?"

"It was sucking the life out of me. My spirit, my creative spirit."

"You an artist?"

"Not really."

"But you have a creative spirit."

"We all do, Mr. Hamilton."

"Call me Harvey."

"Sitting around in a room talking about how important we are. Like seriously, who are they kidding?" Rayanne flicked her cigarette out the window. "We're all just a bunch of lemmings marching on to our death."

"I suppose that's one way of looking at it."

"Any other way is just a delusion. Look at your truck here. It's a gas guzzling pig—"

"That you're riding in," Harvey said.

"Exactly! I'm a lemming; you're a lemming. We're destroying the planet. But the joke's on us because Earth won't die, only we will. We're all going to die and then the earth will just rejuvenate."

"I don't know that it's as bad as all that."

"You work in the oil industry. You have to say that."

"I'm retired."

"See? It doesn't even matter to you because you'll be dead before the rest of us die anyway."

"Rayanne, is this the kind of stuff you talk to your boyfriends about?"

"For shit's sake, Mr.—Harvey, do I look like I have boyfriends?"

Harvey nodded. "Well, no. Not really."

"Well, I do talk about this kind of stuff with my girlfriends."

"You're a feminist?"

Rayanne laughed, "Sure. I'm a feminist."

"What does your mother think about it?"

"She thinks I should get the hell out of Fort St. John."

"I suppose so."

"It's a shit-hole."

"Well now, I wouldn't go that far."

"That's because you're not a feminist."

Harvey laughed. "You got me there."

They were approaching the exits to Spruce Grove. It was getting on, and time to think about stopping for the night. "You ever seen the Vegreville egg?"

"Nope."

"Roman never took you to see the egg?"

Rayanne snorted, "Nooo."

"It's your heritage."

"My grandpa wants dinner on the table at 5:30. He doesn't care if it's cabbage rolls or fried chicken. I don't have a heritage."

"We'll stop by the egg on our way out tomorrow. You should at least get a picture."

"I don't have a camera."

"Your phone should have one."

"I don't have a phone. They screw with your brain cells."

Harvey pulled on his bottom lip. "Well, I think I got a camera in my phone. Your mom would like to see a picture of you with the egg."

"Okay. Why not?" Rayanne said.

"Okay, " Harvey said.

"Do you mind if I sleep in the truck tonight?" she asked.

Harvey looked at Rayanne.

"I'm trying to conserve funds," she said.

Tracy would have a conniption if she knew he was letting a girl sleep in his truck alone. "Rayanne, you know my daughter Tracy?"

She wrinkled her nose. "The one who keeps trying to get my mom to go to church?"

"That'd be her."

"I can't say I know her that well. Sorry Harvey, but if I see your daughter coming I turn the other way."

"Yeah. She's got her own way of moving in this world. But you know, I think she'd have my head if she knew I let you sleep out here. Alone."

"Then, I guess what she doesn't know won't hurt her."

"You could sleep in the room with me."

"That's just weird."

Harvey nodded. "Well I guess. As long as you're comfortable."

"I've slept in worse."

"I'll take us all the way to Vegreville then. Who knows what could happen overnight in Edmonton."

"Sure thing," Rayanne said. "Thanks Harvey."

RAYANNE, NO WORSE FOR THE NIGHT'S WEAR, cavorted around the base that held the world's largest pysanka. "Dude! This egg is awesome!" she shouted. "My people are awesome."

"Stand still or the picture will be blurry," Harvey said.

Ruth would have been put off by Rayanne's odd-ness. It was strange not having Ruth looking over his shoulder at every precious thing, although keeping her box nearby took away some of the sting, no mat-ter what Tracy thought. Harvey figured he'd just keep Ruth with him until his time ran out too and then maybe Tracy could dump the two of them into the Bennett Dam. They had some nice enough times up there; the summer before Tracy started grade one they had a fine picnic at the dam, them dinosaur footprints were something else. But later, Ruth refused to return.

"I don't like what they're advertising is all," Ruth said.

Harvey rolled his shoulders with irritation. "What are they advertising, Ruthie?"

"You know very well."

"Them rocks have been measured by scientists."

"Atheist scientists."

"How do you explain the footprints?"

"There was a flood. And they got spread around."

"Ruthie, I'm not even an educated man and I know better."

"You know better than God?"

"Now, that's not what I said."

"It's a long time in hell, Harvey."

"I just thought you would enjoy a picnic," he said. "We could call Tracy and Dale."

"Let's go to the Beatton then," Ruth said. "I'll call Tracy and you can put some eggs on to boil."

Actually, it would probably be easier for Tracy to dispose of him and Ruth somewhere along the Beatton River, and nicer for her too. She and Dale and the girls might have a nice picnic again.

Harvey closed his phone. "How about some breakfast?" he said. "My treat."

HARVEY'S GUT COULD TOLERATE two poached eggs, back bacon and a glass of skim milk. The girl, on the other hand, could pack it in; three pancakes, three pieces of bacon, three sausages, two eggs, hash browns, toast and coffee.

She stabbed a sausage with her fork and took a large bite. "Have you ever heard of the passenger pigeon?" she said through her full mouth of food.

"Not that I recall." Harvey sprinkled his eggs lightly (lightly!) with salt.

"Pardon my French, but it's totally fucked up." She cut into her pancakes. "They're like the buffalo, but worse." She took a forkful into her mouth and continued, "They travelled in flocks that were so big they would take hours to pass over a place. And they lived like that, you know, safety in numbers. It worked until the humans got them." She took a swig of her coffee, set it down and looked at Harvey. "You know the term stool pigeon?"

"Yeah," Harvey said.

"It comes from the passenger pigeon because one way they had of killing these birds who were like, communists—I mean communal—was to catch a single bird and sew its poor eyes shut. Then, they would attach the sucker to a rope and tie it to a stool that they would hoist into the air and then let it drop back to the ground. When the stool dropped back down the bird would try to land but because it couldn't see it would flap its wings. Then all the other poor suckers would land beside it, the so-called hunters would throw a net over the birds and crush their skulls. Hence, the term stool pigeon."

"Well, you learn something new every day," Harvey said.

"Or they got them loaded on alcohol soaked grain then shot them. I mean what kind of a contest is that?"

"Not much, I suppose."

"Exactly." Rayanne looked at Harvey. "Humans are awful, aren't we," she said quietly. "It's just as well we're killing ourselves."

Harvey scratched his ear, "I don't know about that. Some humans are pretty good."

Rayanne snorted. "As long as you look pretty and shut up."

"I think you got to try to look at it differently."

"Why, Harvey?"

"So you'll feel better?"

"I feel fine."

"It don't seem that way to me."

"Well, Harvey, how would you like to be the one with your eyes sewed shut and thrown up into air as a decoy?"

"I'm sure I wouldn't like it."

"Exactly."

Harvey sighed. Sometimes there was no use in arguing with women.

TO THE SOUTHEAST A STORM CHURNED above the prairie, the clouds, biblical and ominous, converged in a fat mess of indigo and grey. Harvey and Rayanne had been watching the storm rise for the past twenty minutes.

"Imagine waiting for that in your little sod house," Rayanne whispered.

"You like history?"

Rayanne shrugged, "It's okay. I just wish it was different."

"Are there any of them pigeons left?"

"One. It's stuffed and in the Smithsonian." Rayanne lifted her chin toward the dark sky. "Are we driving into that?"

"We're just coming into Maidstone. We can drive in and wait it out if it'd make you feel better."

"If it wouldn't be any trouble."

"No trouble at all."

"I don't like to be nervous."

"There's more than once I've found myself praying through one of them summer storms."

"Are you a religious guy?"

Harvey turned off the highway. "I suppose it depends," he said.

"On what?"

"Well, the way I understand it Jesus put an end to death. You know Ruthie died here but her body lives on in heaven. That sounds good enough to me."

Harvey parked in front of a plain brick and stucco hotel. "How about we go looking for a piece of pie," he suggested. "My treat."

"Sure."

HARVEY GRABBED A MENU and took a seat at a small table near the front window of the hotel. "You know, I just want to go where Ruthie goes is all," Harvey said.

"What if you don't go anywhere?"

"Well then, I suppose I've covered my bases."

Rayanne nodded.

Harvey smiled at the waitress. "Two pieces of apple pie sounds good. I'll have mine with a slice of cheese."

Rayanne wrinkled her nose. "Ice cream with mine, please," she said.

Harvey rubbed his chin. "So, you don't much like history, but you know a lot about it. You don't believe in God and you don't believe in people. It seems to me you're just making things harder than they have to be."

"I believe in people."

"You could have fooled me."

Rayanne turned and looked out the window toward the approaching storm.

IN THE END RUTH LOST ALL HER FAT, weighing less than she did on their wedding day. Of course, in the end she wasn't the kind of thin people aspire toward, her skin hung from her bones while she lay propped against the pillows. She took comfort in Tracy and Pastor Daniel shaking and singing around her sick-bed. Harvey tucked himself into a corner and waited for the moments when he was left alone in the room with his wife.

"Harve?" she called.

"Here." He moved to sit beside her on the bed. "How about a sip a water?"

"I'm sorry if I wasn't as nice to you as I should've been."

"You've been plenty nice, Ruthie."

"When I'm worried, I don't think I say things right."

"You didn't say nothing I didn't deserve."

"I just want to be sure I'll see you again."

"I'm not going nowhere."

"I'm talking about the next life, Harvey."

"Now Ruthie, don't talk like that."

"It's your eternal soul, Harve. I can't be silent."

"You think I'm as bad as all that?"

"Good works aren't enough to save you. We all come short of the glory of God, that's why you have to receive Jesus."

"You want me to receive Jesus?"

"I'll pray on it til my last breath, Harvey."

Harvey brought Ruth's hand to his mouth and kissed it. "I have every intention of following you, darling. So I guess you'd better tell me what to do."

She smiled, and Harvey could see the girl he married again. "You just gotta believe, Harvey. And say this prayer with me: God, I know I am a sinner. I believe Jesus was my substitute when he died on the cross. I believe His shed blood, death, burial and resurrection were for me. I now receive him as my saviour and I thank You Lord for the forgiveness of my sins, the gifts of salvation and everlasting life because of Your merciful grace. Amen."

When he had finished, Harvey lay down carefully beside Ruth. She let her hand fall against his cheek. "We have all fallen short of the glory of God," she whispered, "but now you are safe." Then she closed her eyes and drifted into sleep. Harvey held his hand above her mouth and caught her exhalations in his palm.

RAYANNE CHEWED AT HER INDEX FINGER. "When I was a kid my granddad told me that thunder was really, like, God bombs," she said, keeping her face turned toward the storm. "You know, that God was throwing bombs at us for being lazy and not cleaning our bedrooms. He said lightning could come through the window, and if God saw my room was messy I could be next." She flicked a chewed piece of fingernail to the floor. "It was a good way to get me to clean my room I suppose."

Rayanne turned away from the stormy window. "Anyway, I do believe in people," she said. "I just have to find mine."

"And where do you suppose you're going to find them?"

"I was thinking maybe Vancouver."

"Well then, what the hell are you doing going to Niagara Falls?"

"You offered." Rayanne crossed her arms. "What the hell are you doing going to Niagara Falls?"

"When she married me I promised Ruthie I'd take her."

"I hate to break it to you Harvey, but she's dead."

"Ruth's with me all the time."

"Yeah, in a box full of ashes."

"I believe she's looking down on me from heaven."

Rayanne snorted.

"Why not? We were married for close to fifty years."

"Well then, she can look at Niagara Falls or anything she wants any time, can't she? I mean it's a lot of trouble to go through over a dead person."

"Try saying that after you've been married to someone for fifty years."

"I don't believe in marriage."

Harvey laughed, "You are the strangest girl."

"It's elitist. It serves the patriarchy and positions men and women in gendered stereotypes. It privileges monogamy and romantic love above other meaningful relationships, and when same-sex couples allow themselves to marry they buy into the same horseshit the capitalist consumer culture has been dishing out for centuries."

"Now, I don't even know what you said. But let me ask you this, what about love?"

"Whoever said marriage and love were the same thing?"

"Well, I'm starting to see why you wanted to get out of Fort St. John."

Rayanne threw back her head and burst with laughter. Harvey laughed too, thinking of old Roman Wasalyk, who treated his wife and daughter to a lifetime of kitchen duty. This one must have raised his blood pressure. A spirited girl like Rayanne must've made old Roman spit his false teeth out.

"So, you think you're going to find your flock in Vancouver," he said.

"I've seen them before. When I visited."

Rain was pounding against the café window now and thunder cracked above their heads. Rayanne shuddered.

"You get plenty of rain in Vancouver," he said.

"It's not the rain. It's the thunder," the sky flashed, "and the lightning. Well, I guess I'm going to have to keep my room clean no matter where I am."

Harvey sipped his water and watched the girl break a piece of crust off her pie with her fingers and pop it in her mouth. He felt for her, all alone as she must have been growing up. She was like them pigeons she talked about, the last of her kind, or more likely, the first. It wasn't easy being the odd one out, though he supposed, in the end, it made her stronger. Harvey liked to think he would have had fun raising up a girl like her. Ruth, on the other hand, would have hated every blessed minute of it. But it was no wonder the kid wanted to go to the city, safety in numbers and all that.

Ruth. Sitting in a box in the truck waiting on her man. Dead as a doornail according to Rayanne and, Jesus forgive him, the kid was probably right. Still Harvey wasn't taking no chances, the kid could be wrong too. He wished for the faith of Ruth and Tracy, hell he prayed for it, but so far no good. Why is it Jesus had so much time for one man and so little for another? If Harvey were honest, he'd say the first man had a hell of an imagination reading divine authority into random acts.

It gave Ruthie a portion of comfort to think there was some divine plan in her womb not working right but, sorry Jesus, Harvey guessed it was more likely rotten luck. He just wasn't the type who knew something like that for sure. It was a fact that the only thing Harvey really believed is that actions speak louder than words. And if Ruthie was listening then, by God, she had to know he was trying his hardest.

"How about we just take you to the coast now," Harvey said, surprising even himself.

Rayanne squinted at him. "I thought you were going to take your wife to Niagara Falls?"

"You said it yourself, Rayanne. She's nothing but ashes in a box."

"I didn't mean it to stop you."

There could be little doubt that Tracy would pop a gasket when she found out what he'd done. She'd make him out to be a fool, start on again about him moving in with her and Dale and the girls. He could hear her now: Dad, you don't know whether you're coming or going. So be it. Tracy was foolish enough in her own right.

And Ruth too. She let them pastors fill her head up with shame regarding her own natural self. Lord, she could make him dizzy with her kisses back when they were kids. Her tongue was light and quick and Harvey would never say he regretted marrying her. He loved Ruth right on through til the end. He didn't care if all she was good for was a dry kiss goodnight, and he was happy to just tuck up against her while they slept, but the girl he started life with was gone so fast that sometimes Harvey thought he'd imagined Ruth spraying her hair and coating her lips in pink.

Once, right after she joined her Gospel Assembly, he asked Ruth, "Just tell me, Ruthie, what can Jesus give you that I can't?"

"Hope," she said.

Christ, she went right for the jugular.

Harvey truly believed that good enough was good enough, or he did until Rayanne started to talk about pigeons and romantic love. Nothing was good enough for that girl, and the more he thought about it the more he was inclined to agree with her. Rayanne was full of piss and vinegar and not afraid to say so. She made him think of Ruthie when they were just married, minus the brush cut and plaid shirt.

Well, Harvey couldn't see why he couldn't provide hope to someone, even if hope took the form of a sudden change in plans.

"She never seen Vancouver neither. I expect she'll like the ocean just as much," he said.

"I suppose so," Rayanne said.

"Not all people are arseholes."

Rayanne nodded. "Just about ninety percent, I'd say."

"Give or take five," Harvey answered and signaled for the cheque.

HAPPY BIRTHDAY

1

MY PARENTS LIKED TO PARTY. When I was young they enjoyed a busy social life of curling bonspiels, bridge nights, and nine holes of golf followed by drinks in the clubhouse. Heated arguments between my parents were not uncommon although the bad feelings between them rarely remained. They were happy with one another and, for the most part, they were happy with their lives.

The year my mother turned eighty-three my partner, Lydia, and I were closing in on our first decade together. We were not happy with each other, or with our lives. Assisted reproductive technology had broken us. Clomid unleashed Lydia's bulldog nature and I was inclined to brood. Lydia returned to work after our daughter was born, I remained at home letting the dull business of caring for two children merge with my petulance. Lydia managed a large staff of therapists and student trainees who worked with youth at risk. She resented my cushy days, although she usually loathed to say so and had no desire to stay home with two children under six.

Each evening after work Lydia tucked into a bottle of wine, which she drank until it was empty and she was ready for sleep. I took Tuesday mornings off, while Georgia was at playschool and Henry was in kindergarten, for a clandestine sex date with our insurance broker, a man I'd dated in high school and couldn't resist crawling back into the sack with. My affection for Lydia—and hers for me—had been devoured by sleep deprivation, grudges and the constant demands of two children under six.

2

MY SISTER PATTY BOUGHT A LARGE DAIRY QUEEN ice-cream cake to be served at my mother's eighty-third birthday party. She had two photographs of my mom transferred onto the cake's icing. One was of my mom in her early forties all dolled up for a New Year's Eve party; she was wearing a pink satin dress, matching pink mules and was perched on the side of our brown couch. The second was a more recent snapshot; she was at a mountain chalet with her bridge mates, dressed and drinking for cocktail hour. A gold thread shawl had fallen off her shoulder; she was holding a gin and tonic in her hand. Her loose arms were tanned and ripe with age.

My mother had recently been diagnosed with progressive dementia and we wanted to throw her a party that she might remember, at least for the time being. The sad story of my father's death, his massive heart attack on the golf course when they were playing a half round before a trip to the mountains for a weekend of revelry with friends, was already a tick in our mom's brain. We were hoping to create a reasonable diversion. Two of my sisters, Patty and Jane, were convinced that now we had to treat each event with our mom as though it was her last. "And she'll be treating each one like it's her first," Marg, my third sister, said.

3

AS USUAL, LYDIA AND I WERE LATE. My sisters were crowded around Patty's kitchen island, mixing drinks and organizing chili and garlic toast for supper. Mom's bridge pals were on Patty's oversized sundeck, waiting on whisky sours. The kitchen was teeming with grandchildren and the ones who were old enough to drink were already well into it. It reminded me of those split-cell amoebae slides you could look at under a microscope, the kind they showed on TV with the generic male background voice making sweeping statements. I hate those shows.

Everyone was speaking at once, so our arrival barely registered on the room.

My oldest sister, Jane, hugged me but refused to acknowledge Lydia.

Lydia and I hadn't yet managed to get drinks when my niece Victoria blew through the front doors and the entire party leapt to her attention. Jane's daughter had just returned from Australia, where she had lived for five years. She returned from Australia with an enchanting pattern of speech adopted from the country where everyone is a cunt, even those that don't have them.

"Lord, she's pretentious!" Lydia hissed in my ear.

Victoria was all legs and bountiful red hair. She wore a hand-knit top (yes, she made it herself) that set off her spectacular décolletage. She had ditched her lover, an experimental performance artist, Down Under. She had grown tired of his mood swings and his predilection for his fans, both male and female. Victoria had returned to the fold.

"Kate!" Victoria took me into an expansive hug. "I've got some excellent weed in my bag," she whispered in my ear. "Meet me on the deck."

"I'm pretty much off that shit," I answered. Victoria hadn't been back long enough to notice the toll that motherhood took.

Lydia, tired of being ignored, grabbed a beer and moved in beside mom.

Mom kissed her hand and asked, "Where have you been all my life?"

"Right here beside you, gorgeous."

My mother tittered. Lydia was her girl-crush.

I made for the bathroom. Already I needed to sit alone.

4

MY FAMILY HAD GROWN COOL on Lydia after a party the summer before. Patty was married to a man who knew how to make money, but who was a failure at conversation. At his house, Gary avoided family parties by staying upstairs to catch up on bookkeeping. My mother was already suspicious of Gary's poor social skills, then Lydia got mom hammered on peach bellinis and egged her on just for the hell of it.

"Mary," she said, "you know what Gary's really doing up there, don't you?" Lydia winked but mom was too far gone to notice. "He's watching porn on his computer."

"Don't be an ass," I said to Lydia.

"He wouldn't dare!" Mom took a large swig of her bellini.

"Why else would he spend every family party upstairs?" Lydia asked. "Are we that difficult to be around?"

"I should hope not!"

"I work with porn addicts." Lydia was having a high time.

"Please," I said.

My mother staggered to her feet, "I'm going to give him a piece of my mind!"

Patty looked up from the counter where she was building a salad (she was always building a salad). "What's going on?"

Mom shook her finger in Patty's face. "You may let him get away with it, but I won't be party to such behaviour!"

"What's she talking about?" Patty asked me, while Lydia giggled hysterically.

"Don't be a goddamn doormat!" mom shouted.

"Mom!" Jane took mom's arm. Grandchildren looked on in alarm.

"Look what you've done," I said to Lydia.

"Grandma's mad," Georgia said.

"Let's go get popsicles!" Marg grabbed Georgia and Henry and pulled them out of the room. The older grandchildren followed, impressed and embarrassed by Grandma Mary's outburst.

It took fifteen minutes to calm mom down and by then the party had lost all its charm. "How come Gary gets to stay upstairs?" Lydia asked. "Why doesn't he just bring his work down?" She pointed to Marg's husband Chris, who had been tucked into a corner reading *Dead Ends*, a true-crime story about Aileen Wuornos during the entire brouhaha.

5

I COULD HEAR BURSTS OF LAUGHTER, and Henry and Georgia chasing down the hallway. Someone put on a Celine Dion album and cranked it up.

Then Lydia yelled, "Who put this crap on?"

Great. Just great.

I missed my brother Scott, who, nearly two years into sobriety, had declined to join us for Mom's birthday. There was no argument to be made against his absence; he was in Edmonton to see his kids. Now that he was immersed in a fearless moral inventory, his sisters and mom were always pushing against the bruise of his childhood. Our dad had wanted a hockey player but got a bookish, quiet boy instead, a boy who spent hours drawing elves and magicians. My dad was always trying to toughen Scott up with a wrestling match or a game of catch with balls that moved fast enough to knock a kid out. Our mom never intervened on her son's behalf. Scott hadn't forgiven that.

A few months back I tried to talk to Scott about Lydia and me. He suggested I read *Codependent No More* but I hate that crap talk about surrender and 'God, as you understand Him'. We'd been something back in the day, Scott and me in our Doc Martens, packing our silver flasks and cigarette cases. Scott may not have been tough, but he could talk himself into any pretty girl's bed. He had been a force to be reckoned with, and surrender had not been a part of his vocabulary in those days.

6

I TOOK THE LONG WAY BACK INTO THE KITCHEN, out the front door and along the side porch to the rear deck that faced the man-made lake. As I turned the corner onto the side deck I walked into Victoria, huddled against the wall with Jane and Marg. They were smoking a joint.

It's a fact that our mother hadn't particularly enjoyed raising kids, although she made sure meals were on the table and we weren't covered in filth. For the most part we were left to our own devices growing up, with the understanding, of course, that we didn't embarrass her or sully the family name. No one set out to make our mother angry—only a fool would do that—however, the fear of reprisal did nothing to prevent Patty and Marg from enthusiastic participation in the 1970s disco dance party with its requisite sex and drugs.

Jane was another matter altogether. She was a math teacher turned school board administrator, she rarely got drunk, and she never smoked cigarettes, let alone pot. Each year she maxed out her annual RRSP contributions.

When I stumbled on them, Marg was already wasted; she smiled sweetly, which I should add is totally contrary to her nature. Her head swung between her shoulders. It's a potent mix, grow-op grass and Marg's drink of choice, a concoction of vodka and champagne.

Jane, cool as a cucumber, passed the joint to me, so naturally I took a toke, a large one, and then a few more just to make certain my sisters knew that I had chops; that I'd been there too, and more ably than them.

Jane, Marg and I nodded at each other, smug and brave, although Marg could no longer hold up her head. The pot hadn't hit me yet, but I knew we were fucked. When my sisters headed back to the party I turned to Victoria. "What were you thinking?"

"You're all over forty," she laughed.

Indisputable.

7

I FOUND MARG IN PATTY'S WALK-IN PANTRY, propped against the wall. "I can't move," she said.

"Just go sit down," I told her, "I'll bring you a tea."

"I can't move," she said, like I was stupid.

Marg had never been cut out for pot, not even back when it was weak, full of seeds, and grown by hippies in the interior of BC.

"Take me to bed," she grabbed my arms.

"I can't take you to bed. It's mom's party."

"I can't go out there."

"Jesus, Marg."

"And tell Chris to go to the airport without me."

Marg's third husband was tucked into the great room with his book. Six weeks earlier he had nearly died during bypass surgery. Chris had been smoking cigarettes since he was twelve and drinking a litre of cola a day since 1987, when he gave up drinking hard liquor. His sister, a born-again Christian living in Texas, was flying in that evening so that Marg could return to work without the worry that Chris would die while she was at the office.

"I'm not going to tell him that."

"Then leave me here to die."

"Oh for fuck's sake," my chest was pounding with panic, "I'll get Patty." At that point I would estimate that I had been at my mother's eighty-third birthday party for forty-five minutes.

8

AT FIFTY MINUTES INTO THE PARTY I cornered Lydia. I insisted she stop drinking, that it was imperative that she get the children home safely. "Darling," she said, "we've got at least four hours left before we're going anywhere. You'll be just fine."

"But you won't drink anymore?"

She shrugged. "Well, I'm going to finish this beer."

"And you have to go tell Chris what happened to Marg," I said.

"You're pushing it," she answered, but she made her way over to Chris.

I looked at Jane, vigorously chopping vegetables for salad. She was the kind of cook who took knife-handling classes. The knife was moving at a rapid clip, her fingertips tucked under her knuckles.

Georgia grabbed at my hand, but I shook her off. "Go find Mommy Lydia," I hissed. She turned away and I saw her perfect little bum and her sweet little bobbed hair and called her back. "You're beautiful," I told her. My eyes almost wanted to cry. I covered her face in kisses.

Jane raised her knife and pointed at me. "Wash the grapes," she ordered.

"Go find Mommy," I said to Georgia. Because Jane is first born and I am last born I washed the grapes.

Patty, returned from depositing Marg in her bed, poured herself a glass of wine. "You boneheads," she said.

Infused with anxiety, I started to giggle.

"What's so funny?" my mom asked.

I looked to Jane; she had become the knife, slicing into cucumber without raising her head. No one would dare question the necessity of Jane to be occupied by work. Gourmet cook, gardener, seamstress, Jane had failed at nothing except her marriage.

Jane had been divorced for almost twenty years, her ex-husband Buzz, so called for his resemblance to the astronaut, lived half the year in Palm Springs, California, and was still greatly missed by our mother. He was the first son-in-law, father of the first grandchild, and a dentist. It didn't occur to our mother that he might have had something to do with the demise of his marriage, that his clichéd flings with clean-faced dental assistants might have provoked my sister to leave her husband. In my mother's mind a smart woman didn't leave a dentist over a little fling here and there.

9

"I SAID, WHAT'S SO FUNNY?" mom asked again.

"Yeah, tell us the joke," Lydia called from where she still sat with Chris.

"There's so much unforgiveness between us," I told Lydia.

"What?" my mom said.

Jane swept the cucumber into the salad bowl. "Is this really the time?" she asked.

"Unforgiveness isn't a word, Princess," Lydia said to me.

Princess is the word Lydia likes to use to remind me she's the primary income earner and I'm the slacker who mooches off her bounty.

I set the grapes in front of Jane and wiped my hands on my jeans. "You've just made my point."

"What's going on?" my mother asked.

"Kate is feeling a little paranoid," Lydia told her.

"You take pleasure in being nasty," I said to Lydia.

"Not at all," she answered. "But I have no patience for stupidity."

"Are you calling me stupid?"

"If the shoe fits."

"Enough!" Patty stood between us.

"We're just having a little fun," Lydia told her. "Right, doll?"

"Doll?" I asked.

"It's a term of endearment."

I looked at Lydia, sitting on the couch, one leg casually slung over the other, her arms thrown open, speaking the language of being right at home. She'd learned about those signifiers in the school of social work and now she was practiced at the look of casual detachment.

"I need to walk around the block," I said.

"You need to grow up," Lydia muttered.

"What's going on?" mom asked again.

Lydia moved to join her. "Katie's just going to clear her head."

10

I NEEDED TO CLEAR MY HEAD ALL RIGHT. I needed to dream about punching Lydia in the fucking mouth. Or better yet, cutting her to the quick with my vicious wit, something like, *No, Lydia, YOU are the asshole* or *Lydia, I hate you so much I'd rather fuck a man than you.* I liked the idea of making her cry. I grabbed my bag so I could buy a coke at the service station, maybe the caffeine would sober me up, and I marched away from the house, my chest thumping with the combined effects of twenty-first century weed and revenge fantasies.

Patty's house was a ten-minute walk from the Esso that leads to the highway, and by the time I reached it I wasn't feeling quite so fucked up. I grabbed a coke and a bag of salt and vinegar chips then sat on a random concrete traffic barrier that had been left (presumably) in the Esso parking lot and watched the summer cars swarm the road. It made me want to run across the road and stick out my thumb.

I had hitchhiked around France and Spain in 1989 with an Irish girl I loved, but in Europe drivers were used to backpacking travelers and rides were easy. Nowadays, I routinely drove past hitchhikers—me, and pretty much the rest of Canada. Hitchhiking no longer seemed reasonable. Hitchhiking was like some fantasy past because once it's over, did it ever really happen, or was it simply an illusion I had of my youth? There were no photographs of me hitchhiking through France and Spain. I would never tell my children I had hitchhiked through France and Spain.

11

IT PISSED MY MOM OFF WHEN I TOLD HER I was a lesbian. Right after I spit it out she lit a cigarette and inhaled slowly. After she exhaled she squinted in my direction and told me to leave now. My sister Patty stuck by me and told my mom she was lucky to have a daughter like me. I could have been that serial killer Charles Ing, who happened to be in the news at the time. So, I was surprised that mom took to Lydia the way she did. Well, Lydia had boyish charm and she could hang a light and fix plumbing; not even my dad could do that.

And, I suppose, I was a little hurt that she took to Lydia the way she did. You want your mother to like your partner, but you don't want your mother to like your partner more than she likes you. I have spent too much time wanting people to like me. My desire for approval has shaped everything about me. Even my kids were a vain attempt to give my mother something to say about me that didn't embarrass her. And it's crazy how much you love your kids. Who ever wanted to feel that vulnerable?

12

I DECIDED TO GIVE MYSELF TEN MINUTES across the highway. I'd stick out my thumb and see if someone would pick me up; it would be hysterical, like *Candid Camera* or something. In fact, it was a little terrifying when, after about five minutes, a guy in a cube van pulled over.

Still, I pulled the door open and climbed in.

"Where you going?" He was skinny, pale and freckled. He was about twenty-five and, going by his style of dress, he was a big fan of hip-hop music. His front teeth pushed on top of one another.

I felt a rush of anxiety as I imagined my family singing Happy Birthday and cutting into my mom's beautiful cake. I was at the age my mother was when she happily posed for that New Year's Eve photo. We were so physically alike, my mother and I. And she had her beloved Lydia with her. My sisters would be worried by my absence; they might even call the police. But they would be kind to Henry and Georgia, and mean to Lydia. My mom wasn't going to remember if I skipped out of her party.

"I'm going to Banff," I said.

"You're in luck. I got a delivery in Golden."

I nodded. Giddy with my daring, at a loss for words.

He lit a cigarette. "You want one?"

"No thanks."

"You got family in Banff?"

"I'm going to see my dad."

"Your dad lives in Banff?"

"We scattered his ashes on the golf course."

"Oh." He blew his cigarette smoke out the window. "You better watch out for them elk. They rut on that course."

I turned my phone in my hand. The shit was going to hit the fan when I didn't return. But since Lydia had no desire to be sole custodial parent of two kids, I figured a brief text would do: c u tomorrow. I hit send.

In Banff I was going to rent a room for the night, have a bath and take myself out for a drink. As we drove west across the city I turned my face northward, away from the bright sun, away from my driver. And I let the panic of not being sugar and spice and everything nice sink into my chest. Tonight, when she had to fight to get two kids into bed, Lydia could see how much she'd like life without me.

"You know," I said to the driver, "I wouldn't mind having one of those cigarettes if the offer's still open."

THIS COLD WAR

THE FIRST TIME I SAW CHARLIE BRIGHT he asked me to tie his blue apron. He leaned toward the bar, still sticky with last night's cocktails and cigarettes, and bent his considerable girth toward my fingers. Charlie was a mouth breather. His hair, grazing the top of his collar, could use a wash. Mousy. If you could call anything about a man that size mousy.

The first time I saw Jane Shaw she paused in the door between the kitchen and the bar, pulled a smoke from behind her ear and lit it. "New flesh," she uttered. Her legs were sheathed—which was not too corny a descriptor for Jane Shaw—in zebra-print leggings and black, thrift-store cowboy boots.

She was a natural red head. You could tell by her pink skin, and by her freckles. Jane Shaw was covered from head to toe in freckles. Her T-shirt said FEED THE WORLD and she had cut the collar and sleeves off so that it hung from her shoulder and offered the hope of a glimpse at her nipples, which surely would be rosy in the most classical sense, like those girls in paintings with cherubs. Jane Shaw didn't have to wear a bra.

Jane Shaw poured herself a coffee and spiked it with bar rum. Charlie started to grumble and Jane laughed. Happy as a little girl, she looked Charlie right in the eye and said "Don't fuck with me, Mr. Bright."

And so he didn't, and at the end of the night, to celebrate my first shift at The Brightside Diner, Charlie poured us a half-litre of red wine.

Jane Shaw sat down beside me and we sipped the cheap, thin wine poured from a screw-cap bottle. It was a Sunday, jazz night with the Matt Frank Quartet. Matt Frank's saxophonist was crazy for Jane. He wiggled onto the bench beside her. Jane bestowed her lazy smile upon him then turned to me and I grinned because who wouldn't be crazy for Jane Shaw?

Jane's live-in boyfriend was a beatnik; he wore black and spoke in a slow, measured monotone, like the misery of being alive was a little more than he could bear. He sported a moustache that curled around his mouth to his chin. He was insane about her trysts: there was the saxophonist and, also, a communist; once there was a PE teacher, and, a couple of times, a manager of a nearby restaurant. But Jane Shaw avoided actors like the plague. Actors needed coddling.

Jane Shaw's beatnik walked through the door and raised his eyebrows—a gesture of hello—then the saxophonist turned away from Jane and toward Charlie, who was surveying his littered empire. Charlie rubbed his chin and looked at the beatnik. Jane Shaw yawned and stretched her arms. She winked at me and said, "I'm going to make Charlie put you on Sunday nights. With me."

Two weeks later, at the end of April, I turned twenty-five. Jane Shaw bought me a cardboard crown that said HAPPY BIRTHDAY and we smoked so much weed in the woman's bathroom that Charlie threatened to fire us. That same night I came perilously close to sleeping with a folk singer, who I later married, and later yet divorced.

ONCE, JANE AND I WENT SWIMMING, and I glimpsed her wild red bush. The day was scorching. We met at the Bowview outdoor pool to "languish in the water," as Jane suggested. In the change room we could hardly move for all the kids and their mothers, holding towels around their modest youngsters. Jane had no respect for their decorum and pulled off her jean shorts. She wore no underwear. It was almost impossible not to stare while she casually searched in her bag for her swimsuit. In the pool we floated on our backs and when our hands touched, we pushed away from each other and let the water bring us back together again.

That night, when the heat of August pressed into the small café and Jane and I were in the bathroom sharing a joint, she leaned over, curious I guess, and kissed me on the lips. She tasted a little sour from cigarettes and the rum in her coffee. After she kissed me, Jane Shaw said "Mmmm. Garlic."

I spent the final hour of my shift chewing my lips and forgetting drink orders.

Charlie yelled, "Snap out of it! I don't pay you girls to get high!"

Jane raised her eyebrows at Charlie.

I tried, for a second, to imagine Jane and me at my parents' house for Thanksgiving dinner. Unbearable. My folks had their ideas about love and family, Jane Shaw wouldn't be a part of them. The year I was born my father opened a term savings account so that, one day, he could walk me down the aisle in style.

I delivered a forgotten jug of beer to a table.

SEVEN WEEKS LATER JANE AND THE BEATNIK moved to Marseilles for the winter. The following spring only the beatnik returned. I thought of going to find Jane but I had seen *The French Connection*; I knew all about Marseilles' gangsters. And—honestly, the thought of flying over the Atlantic, I mean if the plane crashed into the water—I just couldn't do it. Anyway, by then I was on the folk singer's guest list.

Two years after that, I heard that Jane Shaw had hooked up with a Spanish diplomat and was living in a French garden apartment. I distinctly remember hearing the news because that was the night I threw an ashtray at the folk singer. It shattered on the wall behind his head. He was incensed and demanded that I take an anger management class. I told him to go fuck himself.

I went to the Brightside Café for a drink. Charlie poured me another lousy glass of wine 'on the house', although I was no longer on staff. He sat down to join me.

"The man's got a wife," he said. "Jane's his girl on the side. Which is just as well. Could you see Jane in a room full of diplomats?"

"No." I shook my head.

"You look like you're having a rough day." Charlie patted my hand. "How about a tequila shooter?"

THEN, IN THE FALL OF 1989, I heard that Jane was travel-ling with a small group of circus performers from East Berlin. They said that she'd taken up with a raven-haired Berliner who travelled everywhere with a fer-ret sitting on his shoulder. Those were heady days for Berliners, and probably for Jane too.

I was happy enough in 1989, a seed had taken root and I was preparing for the joyful days of motherhood. The folk singer and I had come this far, I had learned to bite my tongue and he had learned to forgive and forget. But the images of Germans hacking at the wall with hammers had barely left the evening news when I lost my first baby, a boy, miscarried at nineteen weeks.

After my second miscarriage, my cervix was declared incompetent. I had hoped for a child to for-tify my attachment to the folk singer, whose star was rapidly rising, but I've never had much drive. Nor was I cut out for the physical disaster of pushing out a baby who will not, even with modern medical interventions, survive. We were past throwing ashtrays and spent the next few years in an extended détente where we shared a house but little else. When he took up with his mandolin player I wasn't surprised.

It became clear to me that I wouldn't be having children.

But it got me to thinking about the patterns in my life. Thinking about why I wanted to be the wife of a folk singer, why I was so worried about my parents' good opinion when they worried so little about mine. And, mostly, about why Jane Shaw and I would get so close, then completely lose touch with one another.

The folk singer isn't the only person who said I was too difficult. I can say without a word of a lie that I have no idea what any of the complainers meant. I liked things the way I liked them. Maybe I should have cried when the doctor told me my cervix would not support the weight of a growing fetus. Or, maybe I should have found a way to let myself fuck my husband again after my diagnosis. I know he thinks I blamed him, and maybe I did. I suppose I'm a bit like that old country song, and my cold, cold war is never done.

LAST YEAR, I TOOK IN A GINGER CAT from a rescue society because I was told they were the most affectionate kind of cat. I named him Shaw but I guess a coyote or a car got him because I've seen neither hide nor hair of him since. But he wasn't affectionate; he bit me when I tried to pet him, and he peed in my favourite pink suede flats. I don't think it was beyond that cat to have just moved in with someone else. He had no feelings.

EDDIE TRUMAN

PEOPLE SAID THE WORST THINGS TO HER as soon as they noticed her belly. They told her they didn't sleep for seven years; they told her their sister's baby girl never woke up. They said colic made them want to throw their baby against the wall, but they didn't, thank God, they didn't. They said boys carry low and girls carry high; they told her a larger right tit means you'll have a son. They told her they were in labour for seventy-two hours before caesarean.

No one told her that they shit all over the table.

Daisy's delivery doctor took pity on her. She stood in the bathroom and turned on the taps with the intention of unlocking Daisy's full bladder. She stayed and chatted while Daisy sat on the toilet attempting to pee.

"When the nurses gave him oxygen, his lungs expanded too quickly and so a tear resulted."

"Okay," Daisy said.

We call it a pneumothorax," the doctor said. "It's just a little rip in his lung and as soon as it heals he'll be as good as gold."

Daisy looked at the hunk of shit on the doctor's boot. Her shit. The doctor would go to where doctors go to wash the shit off their boots and realize it was Daisy's shit. Who else's shit could it be?

"If you'd like to pump your breasts the nurses in NICU can give your milk to the baby," the doctor carried on happily. "What are you naming him?"

IN THE END A NURSE, AN EFFICIENT WOMAN named Sarah who explained that her bladder was in shock, catheterized Daisy.

"Oh my, that must have been uncomfortable," Sarah said once she had finished.

"Mmm hmm," Daisy said.

"Well that's that," said Sarah, pulling the disposable gloves off her hands. She dropped the gloves into the trash and polished her hands with sanitizer. Sarah radiated competence. "Do you want to go see the baby?"

The correct answer was yes. Daisy dragged her feet through the wide, cold hallway of the fifth-floor maternity ward. Winter had arrived and was blowing outside the windows, the first storm of the year and not even Halloween. A young woman stood against the wall, crying into the payphone in a foreign language. Her slippers and flannel nightgown were pink and faded. Her dark hair fell down her back in a mess of tangles.

Sarah clicked her tongue, disapproving. "They start them too young," she cocked her head toward the girl on the phone. The girl wiped the snot from her nose with the back of her hand. The nursing-unit clerk shushed her high-pitched complaint and the girl turned toward the wall leaning into the phone.

"Is your husband coming by?" Sarah asked.

"No," Daisy said, then added, "not today."

"Because he's allowed into the NICU, but no one else."

"Okay."

Sarah passed Daisy a yellow hospital gown. "Put this on. They won't let you enter otherwise."

They had passed through the first set of doors where the sterilized gowns were kept. The babies were behind a second set of doors that had been coated in a dark paint so that it was impossible to see into the next room.

"Come on," Sarah pulled open the doors. "I'll take you to him."

Inside the neonatal intensive care unit, babies the size of squirrels were attached to hoses and contained in clear plastic incubators and bassinets. Daisy couldn't avert her gaze from the miniature disasters dressed in pink and blue toques that had been carefully knitted for them by ladies of the Peter Lougheed Hospital's Volunteer Auxiliary. Mothers and fathers dressed in sterile yellow gowns were scattered throughout the ward. Cradling babies attached to hoses or hands stuffed into incubators, they had the appearance of dazed inhabitants of a science fiction movie.

Sarah deposited Daisy against the back wall of the unit.

"There you go," she said. "Baby Clark, good as gold." And she turned and walked briskly away.

The baby lay in a bassinet, his head under a clear plastic dome. Electrodes were attached to his chest and a cuff was wrapped around his ankle. Both led to blinking machines beside his bed. Baby Clark's eyes were bruised and black, like he'd gone fourteen rounds in the ring; well, at least he was in pain, too. Also, there was a surprising amount of red hair plastered to his head. It was impossible to know who he looked like.

"You can touch him you know, it won't hurt him."

Daisy turned toward the voice. A woman in her mid-twenties sat in a cushioned rocking chair cradling a baby in a blue beanie close to her chest; they were skin to skin. Her eyes were large with exhaustion and her kinky hair was flat against the right side of her head. The baby's twin lay sleeping in a pink hat in the heated bassinet next to Baby Clark. The infants were connected to a series of machines by electrodes, plastic cuffs, and oxygen hooked into their noses.

"Babies like to be touched," she said. "It's good for them."

Daisy placed her hand lightly on Baby Clark's unfettered foot.

"You've got a big one."

"Eight pounds, four ounces," Daisy said, running her finger up his fresh calf.

"Count your blessings," the woman said. "Count your blessings."

"The doctor had to stitch me up afterward," Daisy said.

"I hope you're not complaining."

Daisy looked again at the young woman. "I guess not."

"I'm Sandy," she said. She reached a hand toward Daisy but the baby squeaked unhappily and Sandy pressed the baby tight against her bare chest again. "I'd shake your hand but I'm otherwise occupied."

"Daisy."

"That's not a name you hear every day."

Daisy nodded, "My parents are hippies."

"That explains it."

Daisy squeezed her lips between her teeth, then made a popping sound. "Yup."

"Where are your folks now?" Sandy asked.

Jesus the woman asked a lot of questions. "The East Kootneys, I think."

"You think?"

"Well, they're off grid."

"Don't they want to know about their grandson?"

Daisy turned back toward her baby, "I'll send them a card."

"I guess that's thoughtful of you."

"They don't believe in increasing the human population," Daisy said. She was liking this version of her life.

"How do they explain you?" Sandy asked.

"They had me before they formulated their world view."

"Easy for them to say then, isn't it?"

Daisy pulled a chair close to the baby's bed and then sat down. She had no answer for Sandy and so remained silent.

"Has anyone talked to you about the baby blues?" Sandy asked. "Because you gotta watch out for that."

WHEN DAISY CALLED HER MOTHER to say she was pregnant her mother said, "For God's sake, Jean, you're thirty-nine years old, why are you asking me what to do?"

"Daisy."

"What?"

"I changed my name."

"You can't expect me to go along with that," her mother snapped.

"Why not?"

"Because I gave you a perfectly good name."

"I prefer Daisy."

"Your father would be rolling over in his grave."

"Seriously?" Daisy's voice rose.

"It wasn't as easy for me as you think," her mother said.

"You don't know what I think," Daisy said. "And you don't know what my father thought."

Her mother sighed heavily. "Jean—Daisy. Holding onto the past will make you sick."

"I've got to go," Daisy said.

"Wait," her mother said. "Don't hang up, darling. What are you going to do about the baby?"

"Terminate."

"I suppose it's for the best."

"Yup." Daisy's throat tightened.

"Children are a grind."

"Sure," Daisy said.

Like she was reading her mind, Daisy's mom said, "It was different with Little Bill. I wasn't his mother, it didn't matter to me how he turned out. And Lisa has the patience of Job."

"Of course."

"You're still so angry." Her mother sounded hurt.

"Not really," Daisy said softly.

"That's why you changed your name. Lisa agrees with me."

"And she should know."

"She's a nurse, Jean. Of course she knows."

"Daisy," Daisy said.

"Daisy," her mother said.

"Good-bye," Daisy said.

"Call me after the—" Her mother searched for the word, "Procedure. Let me know you're okay."

"Sure."

"I love you," her mother said.

"Yup," Daisy said.

Her mother called three weeks later to ask how everything went. Daisy told her everything was fine. And it was. Daisy did not tell her mother she had decided against termination. It seemed so—permanent. A better plan would be to have the baby and then to find it a new home.

*

"WHAT'S HIS NAME?"

"I don't know," Daisy answered.

"What do you mean you don't know? Everybody knows. This little guy here is Martin and pinkie-pie up there sleeping is Mary, after my grandparents."

"That's nice," Daisy said.

"Because these two are little fighters," Sandy said. "Mary came in at two pounds eight ounces and Martin came in at three pounds one. Now, they're three pounds two and three pounds nine. You see, I gave them strong names." Sandy clicked her tongue loudly. "You gotta think about that sort of stuff. You can't give your baby some weak name. That would be stupid. That would be setting him up for failure. My grandparents are deceased now but I know they're in heaven rooting for my babies."

"How do you know a name's weak?"

"Well, some names are obvious. Like, you wouldn't want to name your baby Adolph. Not that Adolph is so much weak as just ugly." Sandy sat quietly for a minute then spoke again. "Ambrose. Ambrose is a weak name."

"Why?"

"Because it sounds like Rose and Rose is a girl's name. And don't give him a name like Dakota or Dallas because a, they're American and b, no one will ever know if Dakota or Dallas is a girl or a boy, although most would be inclined to think it was a girl and that's not good. At that point you may as well name him Ambrose."

"I need some sleep." Daisy stood up, "I've been up all night."

"You better plan on getting used to it," Sandy said as Daisy walked away.

THE ROOM WAS COLD AND DAISY WISHED she'd thought to buy a nightgown, but she didn't expect to be so long at the hospital, and now with the baby in the special care nursery who knew when she'd get out of the stupid blue gown the hospital gave her. With the flimsy hospital robe belted overtop of the crappy gown Daisy looked like an escapee from the second floor psych ward. Her blanket was ridiculous fake crocheted cotton. Daisy pulled herself close but there was no getting warm.

It was the same dream of her father. His cat Truman was curled in his lap and he was singing, "I'll give you a daisy a day dear, I'll give you a daisy a day. I'll love you until the rivers run still and the four winds we know blow away."

As usual, Daisy was surprised to find him in his chair singing and she said, "I thought you were dead."

He said, "Grab us a beer will you Jeannie?"

Daisy woke soaked in sweat and infused with the melancholy that came with dreams of her father. If only it had been the one where he danced on the sidewalk. That dream always made her feel as if he were someplace better.

Daisy didn't like to think about what her father would say about a baby. He would say: Keep it darling.

*

ANNA, THE SOCIAL WORKER at Adoption By Choice, took the three files from Daisy. "You don't like any of them?"

"I don't like the forty-four and forty-five year old," Daisy said. "If you ask me their ship has sailed."

Anna nodded. "And the others?"

"I don't know. They sound kind of flaky. A little touchy-feely for my taste."

"They've had criminal background checks, several home visits. Flaky is not a word I would use to describe them," Anna said. "Loving, perhaps."

Daisy nodded.

"You know, Daisy, you're in a good financial position. You're certainly old enough—"

"Ouch," Daisy said.

Anna blushed. "I just mean I think you could handle it if you wanted to."

"Want being the operative word," Daisy said.

"Want being the operative word," Anna replied.

"They all sound like they want to be my friend."

"Well, they're inviting you into their family."

"Jesus. Who wants more family?"

"Some of the biological parents here, Daisy, are very grateful for the contact."

Daisy frowned. "Why don't they just keep their babies then?"

"Circumstances," Anna said.

"Circumstances?"

"Most of our biological parents are still kids themselves."

"Right," Daisy said.

Anna stood up, "How about I go get you a few more files?"

Daisy nodded. A butterfly fluttered through her stomach and she placed her hand on top of her belly. She rubbed her palm over the bubble of her stomach; neither slow weight gain nor plenty of fruits and vegetables had done anything to prevent the onslaught of stretch marks. Bringing a new life into the world had seemed a lot more promising twenty-four weeks earlier.

TWO GIRLS WERE JUMPING ON THE BED next to Daisy's. Their mother, dressed in teal-green designer yoga pants and matching jacket, held her newest baby and watched her daughters while their father gathered up a bouquet of balloons that shouted Congratulations! and It's a Boy! The girls were wearing matching GAP skirts and flowered tights. They were the kind of people who thought only a son could carry on a family name. And they weren't doing anything at all to control those girls. Daisy stood up and pulled the curtain around her bed.

She looked at the pump that Sarah had just dropped off. She was supposed to milk herself for the baby boy, and this was important, but Daisy couldn't remember why. Antibodies or something. And there was something about nipple confusion. But Sarah was talking about nipple confusion while Daisy was panicking about saying her husband was working in Saudi Arabia. Why did she have to have a husband anyway? Daisy crawled back under the thin hospital sheets and closed her eyes.

At 4:30AM Daisy shuffled down the hall with a small canister of breast milk. It was a classy colour, she could paint her bedroom or dining room the same colour and call it butter-yellow and her houseguests would admire her good taste.

The nurse plucked the milk from her hands and said, "We just fed him. Formula, of course, because we didn't have this on hand." Another efficient nurse, judgmental even, but then nurses were a pretty heartless lot. Maybe you just get mean wiping asses and cleaning puke all day.

The baby was sleeping. His hair, dry now, gave him the look of being shocked, like his newborn hand had been placed on one of those metal balls that makes a person's hair stand on end. Her teacher brought one into class in grade 10. A Van something-or-other generator. Daisy had placed her hand on it and her long hair and feathered bangs had risen up like wings. They'd all laughed, even Daisy.

"Hello little fella," Daisy whispered. He was dressed in a white undershirt and a plastic diaper. What was left of his umbilical cord had turned black and was clamped in a small piece of yellow plastic. She placed her hand carefully on his tummy. It was warm.

"My name's Daisy," she said. "Don't take it personally, but I don't think I'm cut out for motherhood." She pulled the chair close with her foot and then sat beside the baby's bed. "You know, you're much better looking than the sickly little babies in here. You'll have that going for you.

"I can't tell you much about your dad. He's a bit of a dick. I met him on set. He's a camera guy they brought up from LA for a fucking Honda commercial. Don't ask me why. Producers have an elevated sense of their importance; the man thought he had to bring his own camera guy in. Your dad's married and he's got a couple of teenagers. I don't know why I bothered with him. Some people are emotional eaters; some people are emotional fuckers. But he had red in his beard and I guess I have red somewhere too, which is something I didn't know until I saw you.

"Anyway, your biological grandfather died a couple of years ago, but he was a really nice guy so you have that going for you. Or, maybe, against you. I'm just saying it didn't help him much.

"Your biological grandmother is, well honestly, if you get enough of her genes that should pretty much offset the being too nice worries. And I can't say that I especially like people, I don't dislike people per se, but I guess I don't have any illusions about people. The point is: you could do better than us.

"So, you know, I just wanted to say, it's not that I don't like you. I even brought in my colostrum, which is going to load you up with all sorts of good stuff." Daisy moved her hand down the length of his leg. Strange really, how everything was complete on this baby; everything that he was ever going to have was somewhere on, or in, his body. It seemed impossible that he'd ever been curled inside her, except for the third degree tear into her ass. "And watch out for the sun. You're going burn easily. I'm sure of that."

It was quiet in the nursery. The blue baby next door lay alone in an open bassinet; the pink baby had been moved to an incubator. Jesus, that couldn't be good.

The cranky nurse walked over and began to pull the privacy curtain around the twins. "I imagine when the doctor checks your son today he'll agree that Baby Clark can leave the oxygen tent."

"That's good," Daisy said.

"But don't be surprised if he has to go under the bilirubin lamps."

"What?"

"Jaundice."

"Oh."

"He's a little yellow."

"Right."

"Nothing to worry about."

"No." Daisy lifted her chin toward the closed curtain. "What happened there?"

"She was losing body heat. Her parents are coming in."

"Why?"

"It's a tricky time. They need to be here." She stuck her hands into the pockets of her uniform, bright blue scrubs decorated with teddy bears. "But you've got nothing to worry about. You've got a great, big healthy boy."

"I guess."

"Well, I know," she said firmly. "Now, I'm going to close your curtain too, so baby and parents can have some privacy." She snapped the curtain closed and was gone.

"A word to the wise," Daisy whispered to the baby, "don't piss that nurse off." She leaned into the beige leather chair and pushed against its back until she reclined comfortably. The last thing she wanted was to run into crazy Sandy again.

Daisy heard rustling on the other side of the curtain and muffled crying. She heard Sandy say "It's just not fair."

A man's voice answered "You need to trust in the Lord, Sandy."

Daisy snorted. Of course they were religious. Religion was stupid and religious people bored her. "As if," she whispered to the baby.

He opened his eyes and stared at her.

"I know you can't see yet," she told him. "I'm not dense."

But still he kept staring.

"Save it for your next mother." Daisy closed her eyes. She counted to sixty and then opened them again. He was still looking at her.

"I'm not much to look at."

She could hear the doctor on the other side of the curtain. He was talking quietly, but Sandy began to moan as the doctor spoke. It made the hair on Daisy's neck rise. Daisy blinked quickly to stop the flow of tears. What a shit-show.

She heard the doctor say "As comfortable as possible."

Jesus. Daisy knew what that meant. It meant load your dad up with morphine, hold his hand and sing him Willie Nelson songs until it's over. The doctor continued talking in a low voice.

"How long do we have?" Sandy's husband asked.

"We're not sure," the doctor answered. "Hours perhaps, perhaps a day or two. It all depends upon her. But we'll fix it so you can hold her."

Daisy stepped up beside baby Clark. "You shouldn't have to hear this." She stroked his hand. "Don't pay any attention, little guy." She heard the doctor leave while Sandy continued to weep quietly.

Daisy was never going to get out of here without them knowing she had heard the whole thing. If she were her father she'd pull a flask out of her pocket and offer to spike their coffee, assuming they had coffee.

"Hey Sandy," Daisy said.

"Hey Daisy."

"Can I maybe go get you a coffee? Or a muffin?"

"Oh, don't worry about us."

"It's just downstairs."

"I'd appreciate a coffee," her husband said. "With cream, if you don't mind."

"Not at all," Daisy said. "They make great ginger snaps you know. To keep your energy up."

"Okay. Thank you." Sandy started to cry again.

Daisy pulled back the curtain, "I'm really sorry."

Sandy nodded. "How's your little one?"

"He'll probably come off the oxygen later this morning."

"Praise God," Sandy said. Her husband took her hand.

"Yeah," Daisy said, "I suppose."

"Oh Daisy, who knows what the Lord has in store for you."

"I won't even try to guess," Daisy answered.

"No, don't," Sandy said. "Just receive it. Just receive what you are given."

"So one coffee with cream and one ginger cookie?" Daisy said.

Sandy and her husband nodded.

As Daisy waited for the elevator her breasts tightened and began to tingle sharply. She felt moistness

leak through her gown and robe. Jesus Christ Almighty,
her boobs were leaking. She crossed her arms. Thank
God it was early, she should be able to make it back to
her room to change without anyone noticing the wet
spots spreading across her chest. She was leaking like
a broken bag of milk. It almost made her laugh, or cry,
just like in that Joni Mitchell song. Daisy knew it was
the same release too.

DAISY LAY ON HER COUCH with Eddie asleep on her
chest. She placed her hand on top of his soft spot; its
pulse was almost imperceptible. She probably should
have named him Gabriel or Zachary but Edward
Truman Clark is the name on his birth certificate. No
one names a baby Edward any more. Well, maybe the
English name their kids Edward, or the royals. She let
her other hand tap softly against his back and watched
his lips move in sleep like he was nursing, the way a
dog's dreaming legs run.

BIG FAT BEAUTIFUL YOU

WHEN WE ARRIVED AT THE FUNERAL HOME, Caroline had to sign a paper that they were going to set fire to the right guy. Then she cried because they wouldn't let her cremate Jerry with his glasses on. It would ruin the incinerator. "How will he see?" she asked. Jerry had been dressed in a hospital gown by the coroner and placed in a plywood box. Caroline fussed with his hair, which was clumped with wax or glue or some other accessory to dissection, because even in the end Jerry had been vain about his dark curling locks and she wanted to make sure he looked good when he got to the other side. I resisted asking the other side of what? She placed a note on top of his chest. "I just don't want him to think I'm still mad," she said.

Caroline told me she missed the first call. The receiver was off its base when the phone rang, and besides it was two in the morning. After she saw that the call came from Jerry's sister she went to the basement to reply. When her sister-in-law delivered the news Caroline's knees buckled and she fell onto the futon couch like a soap-opera ingénue. Not that she used the words soap-opera ingénue, but I've known my sister long enough to make an accurate estimation.

It made me blush to think of Caroline crumpling like that. I had the idea she watched too much television, although she claimed it was her last pleasure to watch television police make this difficult world a safer place. While she was watching law and order being restored, she liked to let an Ativan dissolve under her tongue and chew blue fish candies she hid in places her kids would never think to look. "If you don't want an apple you can't be that hungry," she would say when her kids complained about the contents of their pantry.

BY THE TIME SHE WAS TWENTY-SIX Caroline had thumbed across the country four times. Our mother would say things like "I'm at my wit's end." And dad would offer pithy comfort such as "The tree that doesn't bend breaks." Of the boyfriends she brought home to our parents, one was a soft-spoken drug dealer who organized community gardens, another was our former parish priest (after he'd left his order), and the third was an installation artist who came for Christmas dinner and claimed to be allergic to turkey.

Between her cross-country trips Caroline settled in Calgary and hosted a Sunday night jam in a basement speakeasy where she smoked cigarettes and talked dirty. She teased her hair, wore ripped fishnets and Doc Martens, and regularly got laid by boys in scruffy T-shirts who played in lousy bands. Caroline was a great fan of Jack Kerouac. She would end each jam by shouting "Be a crazy dumbsaint of the mind!" Regulars to the event often joined in with her, creating moments that were uncomfortably close to church.

When we were still teenagers in Kelowna, Caroline and I sat in the back seat of our father's peach-toned Mercury Cougar while he drove the family to Saturday night mass. "Whither goest thou, Canada, in thy shiny car in the night?" she lamented.

"What on earth are you talking about?" our mother asked.

"It's Jack Kerouac." Caroline's tone made it clear our mom was an idiot.

"What a bunch of nonsense!" Mom was equally dismissive.

Caroline let her head fall against the car window and muttered, "The only people for me are the mad ones, the ones who are mad to live, mad to talk, mad to be saved—"

"That's enough!" Dad barked.

"Desirous of everything at the same time," she mouthed in my direction.

MY SHRINK'S OFFICE IS LOCATED in a century house near the downtown core. I wait quietly outside the closed door of her office until she is ready for me and I keep my eyes down when her previous client walks past. Inside her office there is a small Zen fountain, an imagistic stone carving of a large-bottomed woman, and a dream catcher in the window. Her shelves are lined with books like *The Dance of Anger, The Courage to Heal, Talking Back,* and *The Essential Rumi.*

"Tell me about your childhood," she says.

"It was long," I tell her.

"Tell me what you mean by long."

I'm not sure what she expects me to say. No terrible event occurred. "I kept waiting for something exciting to happen."

"Did it?" She's using her passionless voice. The one that's supposed to tell me she has no opinion on the matter.

"Not to me."

"Tell me about that," she says.

I shrug, "I had a telescope."

She doesn't take notes and so her fingers are constantly at work pulling and pushing against one another. She pauses, for effect I suppose, or because she's expecting a terrible confession. "And?"

"I was an amateur astronomer. I wanted to discover a comet."

"You did?" She is genuinely surprised.

Her surprise compels me to go on, to prove it. "The Bayeux Tapestry records Halley's Comet."

"Oh yes..." She's lost.

"When I was a kid, I did a report on Halley's Comet. Comets are like celestial outsiders."

"Oh yeah?" She nods and pulls her fingers.

"You know," I say, "they're way out on the edge of the solar system and then sometimes they get pulled into a gravitational force and begin their orbital path around the sun."

"And who are you in this orbital equation?"

"I'm the girl with the telescope."

"The witness." Her tone remains passionless, but she's sitting up, more alert. "And how would you describe Caroline in this context?"

This is the thing about shrinks; they're always looking for molehills to turn into mountains. "Caroline wasn't interested in astronomy."

"It's very symbolic, your search for a comet."

Like I need to pay someone eighty dollars an hour to tell me that. "It was a school assignment," I say.

"Your sister was like a comet flashing through your universe."

I think I'm going to fire her. "My sister," I tell my shrink, "wanted to lead by example."

"But you weren't a follower."

"Not for want of trying."

"And how did that make you feel?" She leans toward me with her hands resting on her knees, like she's my friend.

"You know," I tell the shrink, "I didn't come to see you because of my sister. My sister is my best friend."

The shrink nods. "You came to see me because you believe you have intimacy issues."

I cross my arms across my chest. "Precisely." I'm never coming here again.

CAROLINE GOT THE NEWS ABOUT JERRY on the Saturday of the May long weekend. I was in Banff with my girlfriend, trying to resuscitate the dead beast of our relationship, which we had been dragging around for over a year. Caroline wanted me to come home, to help her tell the kids. My girlfriend didn't expect me to stay, but it was, she pointed out, indicative of our situation. Caroline, she said, was always going to be my first priority. I packed my bag and paid a cab driver $250 to get me back to Calgary.

SIX WEEKS AFTER JERRY'S FUNERAL is a warm Friday night and I'm spending the weekend in the suburbs with my sister. I find Caroline on her front steps. She is smoking a cigarette, a bottle of Pale Ale between her feet. "I'm thinking about joining a gym," she says. "I could go while the kids are at school." She takes a long drag on her cigarette, looks down the hill that forms her street. "I have to get a job."

Caroline is jumpy. She emanates panic; it's like her temporary atmosphere. I drop down beside her and take her hand like I know what to do. "You've got a bit of time," I say. Caroline drops her weight against me. "You have no idea how many times I wished he was dead," she squeezes her eyes closed.

*

THE SUMMER BEFORE GRADE NINE, I spent most days at the lake. Sarson Beach was at the end of a long road that wound through houses built on a former apple orchard. Caroline had graduated to guys with cars; she would disappear into sedans and trucks cast off by parents and driven by suntanned boys with names like Craig and Derek. I hung out with a gangly boy named Malcolm Cameron, who could burp the first two lines of *Oh Canada*.

Caroline assumed we went off to make out in some bush somewhere, but instead we were united by the unspeakable strangeness we felt. We didn't have words for our ill-placed desires, or our inability to follow the beautiful boys and girls who conformed to the rules of attraction. We would lie with our heads touching, fingers intertwined and confess to one another our strangeness.

I admitted to Malcolm about the relentless silence in our house, how the only words my parents spoke to one another were "pass the salt" and "pick up some toilet paper on your way home." Unless, of course, we had company.

He told me about his family's annual reunion on the farm in Saskatchewan where his grandparents still lived and men wore caps and drove tractors and slapped him on the back. "I'll bring you back some rye," he promised.

"Rye is gross."

"The grass, stupid."

I slapped his hand away. "Don't call me stupid."

"I meant it in a charming way." He rolled over onto his stomach and groaned. "I don't want to go."

"At least you get to fly." Malcolm's dad had his pilot's license and the family flew in their own Cessna when they travelled to Saskatchewan.

"It's still boring," he griped.

"Malcolm, you are the only person in the world who would complain about flying in a private plane to a family party."

"I wanted a jet."

"Jesus, you're hopeless," I said. Malcolm giggled.

Two days later Mr. Cameron crashed his little plane en route to Saskatchewan. Malcolm, his older sister Sally, his parents and baby sister were killed on impact. I heard about it on the TV news. My mother clicked her tongue and said "Thanks be to God it was fast."

"How do you know it was fast?" Caroline asked.

"Well, Caroline, the news reports they were killed on impact."

"What about while they were falling?" Caroline was indignant.

"What are you so worked up about?" mom asked.

Caroline glared at me. "He was your friend. Don't you even care?"

"Oh dear, he was in your class?" Again, mom clicked her tongue.

"Stop clicking your frigging tongue!" Caroline yelled at mom. "Show some respect for the dead!" And then she stormed out of the room.

"God give me patience," my mother uttered.

I cared, but what was I supposed to do?

A few weeks later, the Cameron house and all their earthly possessions were listed for sale. School was out for the summer and anyway no one talked about shit like that. But I couldn't get those burly uncles Malcolm feared and loved out of my head. I imagined their wives crying out with horror and grief. I would lock myself in the bathroom and practice expressions of anguish, trying to find the place where Malcolm ceased. And in the fall, since nobody likes a whiner, I quietly began school.

That was the year Caroline invited me to the smoke pit to hang with the grade elevens. "You're cool enough," she said. "Besides, you'll be with me."

I would stand beside my sister and smoke poorly, without inhaling. Caroline was usually curled around some boy, oblivious to me and everyone else in the smoke pit. So, I would stand there silently, stupidly, either blowing smoke out too fast or holding it in too long. One lunch hour Caroline took pity and gave me a lesson in the proper inhalation of cigarettes.

"Just breathe it in like air," she instructed. "And then blow it out again but keep your lips tight."

I took in the cigarette smoke and then exhaled.

"Oh fuck," she laughed. "You are such a joke."

It took me seven cigarettes to figure out how to inhale. I spent the rest of the afternoon huddled in the girls's can puking my guts out. I didn't return to the smoke pit. Instead, I tried to teach myself to burp, as a tribute to Malcolm, and I considered going after a real boyfriend, but both tasks filled me with such gloom that I resigned myself to making the honour roll and keeping my parents happy.

The following New Year's Eve, when I opted to stay home, Caroline complained, "I've lost you to the dark side."

I shrugged. I couldn't tell her I hated watching her get wasted and make out with guys. "I don't want to miss Dick Clark."

"You scare me," she said. Then she danced out the door singing "Only the good die young, oh baby, only the good die young."

Such misery and joy in her presence.

EIGHTEEN YEARS LATER, when Caroline was three months pregnant with Sam, she brought Jerry to our parents' thirty-fifth wedding anniversary. By then our parents had given up all hope of grandchildren; Caroline was already thirty-four and they wouldn't abide with the idea that I might bear them a baby. They accepted me—the tree that doesn't bend breaks—but radiated disappointment whenever I brought a girl-friend home. Jerry was the remedy, and my parents—in spite of his shaggy hair, converse sneakers and pro-digious drinking—practically wept with relief when he walked through the door.

Our mother twittered around Jerry, bringing him toast and coffee in the morning while he had a smoke on the sun deck. Caroline and I stood in the kitchen watching her fawn.

"Her prayers have finally been answered," I said.

"Do you like him?" Caroline asked.

"I don't know him well enough to say."

"He really loves me."

"I really love you," I answered.

"And you'd be a perfect husband. If you weren't a girl, and my sister."

I shrugged. "You win some, you lose some."

Our parents uttered the words *son-in-law* at every opportunity, while Caroline grew enormous with Sam, each inch of her body swelling to accommodate the baby. Once she gave birth, Caroline's wildness settled onto her hips and after she delivered Mabel she pulled her dark hair into a ponytail and grew large. Jerry paid the bills laying out posters at Quick Print City, but he was sex, drugs and rock and roll right through to the end.

"WISHFUL THINKING," I SAY TO CAROLINE "did not kill Jerry." The early evening air is cloying; I can hear the raised voices of Sam and Mabel drift from across the street. Hide-and-Go Seek. My sister is still ringing with surprise at the turn her life has taken. Beautiful Caroline, hips pushing against the seams of her navy skirt, breasts and belly rolling through her T-shirt stamped with Japanese characters, lime green toe nails, bare feet.

"If only we still smoked pot," she says.

*

JERRY DIED ALONE. I mean it's hard to imagine you die any other way, even in a crowded room, but Jerry died by himself in a shitty little bedsit, and if it hadn't been month-end and the rent hadn't been due who knows when he would have been found. His room was littered with makeshift crack pipes—empty Bic pens stuffed with steel wool. His guitar was propped against the bedside table, notes scribbled on the back of collection notices and cheque stubs were scattered across his bed. Due to his loose junkie script it was difficult to know if the song he was writing was titled "Failing" or "Falling". At any rate, the lyrics, if they can be called that, were incomplete and fluctuating between remorse and self-pity. At the best of times Jerry was a lousy songwriter, being more suited to thrashing about on a stage than expressing any meaningful emotion.

Caroline placed Jerry's lyrics in an envelope. She planned to deal with them later, bequeath the bits to her children, or destroy them. After all her anger, and Jerry's denials, she was unsure how to proceed. For the first time that I could recall Caroline wanted to follow a prescribed set of instructions, but the etiquette manual on burying your drug addict was not in print.

I SAW JERRY JUST BEFORE THE LONG WEEKEND. He was waiting outside of my office. He was looking for money.

"I wouldn't ask if I had anywhere else to go," he begged. His left front tooth was missing.

"What happened to your tooth?"

He shrugged. "You should see the other guy."

"Caroline's going to have a nervous breakdown." I sounded accusing.

"I know I'm an asshole," he answered. "You don't have to tell me."

"I can't give you money, Jerry. Caroline would kill me."

His hands jerked through his hair. "Don't make me beg."

He was pathetic. "Don't *ever* ask me again."

"I won't. I won't." He clasped my hands. "You're a good sister-in-law. You're a good woman."

I gave him a hundred and fifty bucks. I don't know why. Thirty-six hours later Jerry was dead.

TOMORROW WE ARE TAKING JERRY'S ASHES to Elbow Falls. Caroline wants to dump them in the river at the spot where he proposed to her, when they believed the future was all good things to come. We're bringing a picnic and we'll take snapshots of Sam and Mabel on the big rock where they were photographed as babies.

She tells me that mom called to make sure we obey God's law in the dispensing of Jerry. "No fucking way," I say.

"I told her you were doing a Wiccan ritual," Caroline says.

"Wiccan?"

"She thinks all lesbians are Wiccan. Uncle Gordon sent her some web-link." Our mother fills hours each day surfing the worldwide web while our father naps through CNN. They eat canned soup or beans for lunch and chicken for dinner. Dad uses his *old back* as an excuse to sleep in the spare room. Their conversations remain limited to mail reports and grocery lists.

"Bless her little soul," I say.

Caroline repeats, "Bless her little soul." She points her toes toward the sidewalk. "Let's drop Ativan and watch *CSI Miami*."

Mabel runs up the sidewalk, waves at us then darts along the side of the yellow bungalow across the street. Caroline yells "Ten minutes!"

Mabel throws up her hands, presumably exasperated, then races off to a new hiding spot. "I used to know how to have fun," Caroline mutters.

THERE IS A PLACE I GO AFTER WORK sometimes for a martini and calamari. It fills up with students from the art school and they all have phone cameras with which they document their every action. I blame reality TV, not that there's really anything to blame about kids watching themselves. But I wonder if their documentary will give them comfort down the road, I wonder if everything must be remembered. Maybe, like Jack Kerouac said, we have to accept loss forever.

At forty-five, my sister is fifty pounds heavier than she was in her twenties. You could say her volatilities have evaporated and now she is simply ordinary, because Caroline is like one of those comets that travel fast enough to enter and leave the solar system with almost no attention. I guess I am the witness who noticed the collision and subsequent disintegration of the marvellous light.

I have a picture of Caroline in my mind; she is sixteen, her jeans so tight you can see the outline of her underwear. She is holding a Player's Light in her right hand. Her head is tipped toward the sky, circles of smoke from her lips stretch and curve into complicated tails.

ACKNOWLEDGEMENTS

SOME OF THESE STORIES HAVE APPEARED in *filling Station*, *Grain Magazine*, *Plenitude*, *Prairie Fire*, and *The Puritan*. Thanks for giving my stories a home.

I am very grateful to my mentors and fellow students in the University of Guelph Humber Creative Writing program who helped shaped this book. Your input and direction has been invaluable. In particular I would like to thank Michael Winter and Kathryn Kuitenbrouwer.

Thanks to John Metcalf, Dan Wells and Tara Murphy. I'm pleased as punch to be working with you.

Elisabeth de Mariaffi, thanks for the early reading of stories that needed help.

Thanks to MJ, Burke, Debbie, Sue, Mike, Danny and the rest of my family for the support and the fodder. A special thanks to Martin Cullen for the northern BC geography refresher.

Thanks to Luke and Claire for jumping into the big move with me, and to Mark, for coping with it.

Sharon, Melanie and Jodie Stevens, Kathy Dodd, Joni Clarke, Sharron Toews, Lizzie McGovern, Alex Patience, Laura Parken, Anne Loree, Suzette Mayr, Rose & David Scollard, Lisa Scott, Sharon McCartney, Ayelet Tsabari, Tanis Rideout, Aga Maksimowska, Laurie Graham, and Elisabeth de Mariaffi—thanks for being there (and here).

Helen Humphreys, I am so grateful for your love, but also for your excellent feedback and delicious meals.

John Lefebvre, being on your payroll is such a great blessing. Thank you every day.

NANCY JO CULLEN is the author of three collections of poetry. She has won the Writers' Trust Dayne Ogilvie Prize for Emerging Gay Writer and has been shortlisted for the Gerald Lampert Award, the Writers Guild of Alberta's Stephan G. Stephansson Award, and the W.O. Mitchell Calgary Book Prize. She holds an MFA in Creative Writing from the University of Guelph Humber. She divides her time between Toronto and Kingston.